SOMETIMES LIFE CAN

HOME
GAME

Stephen R. Denison

outskirts
press

Outskirts Press, Inc.
http://www.outskirtspress.com

ISBN: 978-1-9772-5770-3

Cover Photo © 2022 www.gettyimages.com. All rights reserved - used with permission.

Outskirts Press and the "OP" logo are trademarks belonging to Outskirts Press, Inc.

PRINTED IN THE UNITED STATES OF AMERICA

Praise for HOME GAME

I love baseball! And I really loved reading Steve Denison's first novel, *Home Game.* The book captures the spirit of baseball at its roots—minor league ball in the South—but the story is much more than that. The author, with his personal experience in college and professional baseball, dives deep into the hearts and lives of the characters, giving readers a behind-the-scenes look at both the joys and tribulations of aspiring ballplayers. It›s a heartwarming story that leaves the reader wanting more.

Carl McCullough

#1 Best-selling author
"Sid and the Boys:
Playing Ball in the Face of Race and Big Business"

ACKNOWLEDGMENTS

Home Game is my first novel. Whether it is my only one remains to be seen. While I had no doubt in my ability to write a book with a baseball theme, I also quickly realized I had no idea on how to get *Home Game* published, let alone marketed with reasonable chances of sales success.

My first efforts involved trying to find an agent who represented authors with books covering a sports theme. Being a first time, unknown author I found that my "Thank you, but not interested" replies (when I got a reply), were the only answer I would get.

I had read about authors who had successfully published their book through independent publishing companies. I interviewed a number of these companies and found a wide range of pricing, publishing options, and marketing support. I finally settled on Outskirts Press and could not be happier with my decision. From my initial call for information, through submitting my manuscript, designing a cover, and discussing marketing plans, each of their team members have been professional, responsive, and sincerely interested in my success. A sincere thank you to Outskirts Press.

I received tons of ideas from my local Rock Hill, SC writers club as I worked on improving my story. Once finished, my editor Melanie McCullough found more areas that needed cleaning up, making me almost feel like a real author!

During the editing and publishing process, I received

encouragement from my good friend (Melanie's dad, and also first time novelist) Carl McCullough, #1 Best-selling author *"Sid and the Boys: Playing Ball in the Face of Race and Big Business"*. Without the support and push from Team McCullough, I'd probably still be wondering what to do next. Thank you, Team Mac!

And finally my personal home team support in writing *Home Game,* my wife and companion for over 45 years, Pam (aka Grammie Pammie). The first to review my initial chapters and urge me to keep going. Love you, Grammie. It's been quite a ride, hasn't it?

1

LAST GAME

He knew by now what his repaired shoulder could handle. Tonight, in the cool Asheville evening, the dull ache would not be going away. The tall blond hurler got up from his seat in the Greenville Braves bullpen and studied the action on the playing field. He was Greenville's top relief pitcher. It was time to get ready. The knot in his stomach tightened as he rotated his arms around his body, trying to stay loose. *I just might get in this one.*

"Man, what do you think, Brett? Has the rookie been pitching from the stretch all night or what?" The question came from one of Brett Davies' bullpen buddies, assistant coach Frankie Simmonetti.

"Give him a break, Frankie," Brett said with a smile, as he continued to stretch. "He just gets to Greenville this morning, takes his bags out of his car in time to put 'em on the bus for Asheville, and then Skipper tells him he's starting our last game of the year."

The final game of the Southern Association minor league baseball season had drawn a nice Friday night crowd to the Asheville ballpark. The Greenville Braves had battled the Tourists, a farm club of the Colorado Rockies, for seven innings. Frankie looked out on the field as the Braves, clinging to a one-run lead, took their defensive positions in the bottom of the eighth. "Yeah, you're right... a real pucker tester for sure. I guess we should be glad he's only walked five. Of course, he balanced that out with two wild pitches as well."

Ricky Jackson, the young lefty pitching for Greenville, had just been called up from Atlanta's Class A team in Rome, Georgia. It was his first game for the Double A team and he was doing himself proud, giving up just three runs on the night, despite allowing eight hits and five walks.

"Frankie, he's a kid," Brett said. "How old is he . . . twenty? And on top of that he's a lefty; I think we should be glad he's getting the ball over the plate."

Just then the bullpen phone rang. Before the other players could react, Frankie grabbed the receiver. He knew his job, and that included never letting the phone ring more than once. "Yeah?" he bellowed into it. "OK, I'll tell him. I know. . . get ready quick."

Brett had his jacket off and was reaching for his glove before Frankie hung up.

"Davies. Warm up now!"

"Ease up Frankie, I'm right here. Give me ten throws, and I'll be ready."

"OK, make it fast. Skip doesn't want the kid to ruin his evening. Two get on, you're in."

"Only two? I was hoping we could have the bases loaded. Makes the last game more interesting for the fans that way." Brett looked up into the old grandstands. Even though it was a brisk, damp night in the Blue Ridge Mountains, most of the crowd was still there. *Must be a fireworks night.*

He worked quickly while keeping one eye on the field. Jackson managed to strike out his sixth batter of the game to lead off the inning. *Youth is amazing.* Brett struggled to get loosened up for one last time. *If only I hadn't torn my shoulder up. I never used to have these problems.*

The second hitter lined a single to left field and Brett, mindful of the two base runner limit, threw faster to be ready. The next Asheville batter ripped a shot up the middle. Brett prepared to go into the game. But the Braves shortstop, Felix Cardenas, dove to his left snagging the ball in the webbing of his glove and then quickly flipped it to second baseman Matty Boyd for the force out. Brett took a few deep breaths. There was no doubt in his mind why the Braves were bringing Cardenas up for the final month of the big league season. *But why not me?* Brett frowned and tried to get the thought out of his mind. *I'll find out soon enough when I get down to Atlanta and meet with Morey.* Before he could begin throwing again, the Braves got the final out of the inning as the Tourists batter hit an easy pop fly to right. The phone rang and Frankie grabbed it. "OK, Skip. I'll tell him." He turned around, but Brett already had his jacket on and was toweling the sweat off his face. "I know Frankie. Same thing next inning, two base runners, and I'm in."

The Braves went down 1-2-3 in the top of the ninth. They returned to the field with their one-run lead, needing just three more outs for their final win of the season. Brett took his jacket off and strode to the bullpen mound as the first Tourists batter came to the plate. The cool night air had already tightened his weakened muscles during the short time he was sitting. The dull ache remained. Even though Brett had worked diligently in rehab after the surgery, he knew he was not, and probably never would be, the same again. *Good thing I'm older and smarter than all these kids. I'm gonna need it to get through this night.*

Jackson's luck had run out. After getting the first batter on a pop fly, two sharp line drive singles by the Asheville lead off and number two hitters put runners on first and second. As Braves Manager Jimmy Graham headed to the mound to rescue the rookie, Brett didn't need to wait for Skip's signal to the bullpen. Turning to grab his jacket, he wiped his face off with a towel, picked up his glove, and started the long trot in from the right field bullpen. Brett had made it a habit long ago to always jog to the mound. Whether it was from the dugout or the bullpen, he wanted to get there fast and start throwing. *Particularly tonight. Let's get this over quick.*

Ricky was still waiting on the mound when Brett arrived. It was obvious he wanted to hand the ball to his older teammate.

"Great job, Ricky," Brett said.

"Thanks, Brett, go get 'em." Ricky turned to walk off the mound and was surprised by the nice ovation from the hometown crowd.

Brett looked around in the stands as he put the game ball in his mitt. *Darn fireworks. Everyone's still here.*

Graham looked him square in the eye. "OK, Brett, you've been here before. We're up one run, got one out, and runners on first and second. Keep the ball low and get a ground ball. Billy and Doug will protect the lines at first and third base, but I'm going to keep Felix and Matty back at double play depth. Get us a ground ball, and we'll head home to Greenville."

Brett smiled, "You got it Skip--nothing to it." He looked at his catcher, Jose Valanova; and they went over the signals, the usual stuff, fastball, curve, and change up. Home plate umpire, Teddy Brubeck, joined the conversation. "You got eight pitches if you need 'em, Brett."

Brett nodded, "I will tonight, Teddy, thanks." This was the first year that Brubeck had umpired some of his games. Brett had been impressed with his consistency and hustle. Teddy would one day be a good major league umpire. *Another youngster on the way up.* He began taking his warm-up throws with Jose.

The number three hitter for the Tourists was a big left hander. Brett had faced him before and knew he sat on the fastball, just waiting for one to drive. *Nothing too good for you tonight, big fella.* Brett went with his fastball on the first pitch, managing to place it just on the outside part of the plate so the batter fouled it off. A curve and two fastballs later put the count at two balls and two strikes. Brett looked in at Jose and shook him off until he got the curve signal. Brett took the stretch, checked the runners, and then came straight over the top with his curve, hoping to put enough snap on the release so the ball would break straight down as the batter swung over it. Of course, if he didn't get enough spin on the ball, the result would not be good...a hanging curve that seems to sit there in mid-air saying, "Hit me!"

Brett put all he had on the break, but it wasn't enough. The big lefty's eyes lit up, and he smashed a shot down the right field line. Brett's mind raced as he followed the ball. *Great, not only do I not save the game for Ricky, I lose it for me.* A sure double, the speedy runner on first would no doubt come around for the winning run.

But Braves first baseman, Billy Roberson, dove to the line behind first and came up with the ball. Brett's momentum from his follow through had already carried him toward that direction, and he raced with all his might to get to the bag before the runner. It was close, but Brett caught the toss from Billy and stepped on first base a split second before the batter.

Now there were two out, but runners on second and third. Brett knew what was coming and reluctantly glanced over to his manager sitting in the Braves dugout. It made good baseball sense to walk their clean-up hitter to load the bases and set up a force out, especially since he led the Asheville team in home runs. Still, Brett had never liked the strategy. All it would take would be a little wild streak on his part, and the tying run strolls home. But Graham gave the signal to put the batter on and Brett obeyed, tossing four balls wide of the plate to Jose. Three on, two outs, one run ahead.

The next Tourists' batter strode confidently to the plate, as the crowd's roar echoed in Brett's ears. He recognized him as the Rockies number one draft choice from the previous season. The big guy had spent a year and a half terrorizing pitchers in the A leagues and had only been in Asheville since mid-July. Brett had seen the stats of the muscular right-handed hitter and knew his output had not diminished since arriving in town. The crowd was on their feet now, cheering and clapping their hands, certain that the winning hit to end the season was about to happen. *I've got to be careful. Nothing too good, but no way do I go 3-2 and have to give him what he wants.* He looked at Jose for the signal.

"Come on, big man. One more out." Brett could see Jose's white teeth shining through his mask. They had been through a lot together, arriving in the Braves organization in the same season five long years ago. *When we were a lot younger.* He looked in for the sign and took his stretch. Working with care, he struggled with his aching arm. Somehow, he managed to get to a count of two balls and two strikes.

There's no way I can throw it by him, and my overhand curve sure isn't fooling anybody. Brett was still winded from racing to first base to get the second out, when his fatigued brain logged in with a startling revelation. He had never faced this young phenom before. *That means he's never batted off me.* Brett took a deep breath, now confident on what to do. Before taking the rubber to get the sign from Jose, he stared in at his catcher. Reaching his right arm out parallel to the ground, he brought it across his waist as if stretching the arm and shoulder muscles. All the while he kept his eyes on Jose who was now nodding his head, a large smile flashing through the bars of his face mask. Brett looked in for the sign as Jose stuck two meaty fingers down, pointing to the outside part of the plate.

He studied the young superstar as the noise in the stadium continued to build. It was the last game of the season. No one was going home early. Brett rubbed the ball up one more time, placed it in his glove, and then ran his pitching fingers over the sweat that had somehow accumulated on the back of his neck on this cool August night. Nothing illegal, just enough moisture to get a good sticky grip on the ball.

He drew to the stretch, eyed the runners, and with all his strength pushed off the rubber with his back leg. But instead of stepping toward home plate, he changed the direction to a location slightly to the right, halfway between home and third. Dropping his shoulder, he fired the ball sidearm across his body with a quick snap of the wrist, aiming for the hitter's rib cage. Brett could only pray that this time he had put enough spin on the ball.

The young slugger's eyes widened as the ball came hurtling toward him. He only flinched for a split second, but by then it was too late. The ball took a sharp turn a few inches before it was to slam into his side, and then streaked across the outside corner of home plate. Umpire Brubeck called strike three.

Jose was the first to reach him, playfully hugging Brett and pounding him on his back. *"We did it Brett, we did it."*

His other Braves teammates soon followed, and he was engulfed by their cheers and more pounding as they sought to congratulate him for his game-saving performance. It was all he could do to take a deep happy sigh of relief, smiling as he was pummeled from all sides. *Man, I love it when I can do that!*

2

BIG LEAGUE FAMILY

Being the last game of the season, Brett and his teammates did not take long to savor the hard-won victory. In record time they showered, dressed, and raced to their team bus, throwing equipment and other gear into the stowage compartments. Brett plopped down into his usual seat, tired but happy. It was the "cool of the evening," a time to reflect on proud accomplishments of the day. He closed his eyes and tried to rest as the bus rolled along the highway on the sixty-mile drive back to Greenville. Music from his teammates' iPods, along with shouts from winners and losers among the never-ending card games filled the bus. This long hot season had been a successful one, but everyone was glad it was over. Now they could head home to family and friends.

But not Brett. While tonight's game had been the last of the season for Greenville, it was the start of a busy Labor Day weekend for him. One that he hoped would lead to long-awaited answers about his future in the Braves' organization. He stared out the window into the dark night. Sleep was impossible. He had been so close to success before he hurt his shoulder. *What if I can't play anymore? What if they don't want me? What will I do then?*

"What's the matter, Brett? You seem kind of troubled."

Brett looked up to see his manager, Jimmy Graham, standing over him. "Ah, Skip I'm OK--I guess. All right, I'll admit it, I'm bugged they didn't call me up to Atlanta after we're done here. I mean Jessie and Felix had great seasons. They deserve to go. I just thought I did well enough to..."

"You did, Brett," the manager assured him. "You had a heck of a season. Thirty- two saves and an ERA under three. No one expected you to do that, especially after– well, you know what I mean."

"After what? After missing all of last season? After the surgery on my shoulder? After all those rehab sessions? Heck, those hurt worse than when I tore up my shoulder in spring training." Brett stopped. The memory of all he had gone through was still painful. *What's going to happen now?*

Jimmy looked Brett in the eyes. The manager had played or coached professional baseball for more than forty years. He had seen it all and knew when one of his players was feeling down. "Brett, all I can say is my reports on you to the big club were pretty positive. I think we both know your fastball's not what it used to be, but you've become a pitcher, not a thrower. Your control has been great. Keeping it low, getting a lot of double play balls. That's what we need in our top relievers. I don't see why you couldn't do that someday soon in Atlanta."

"Thanks, Jimmy," Brett paused. "I called Chuck this morning. He told me I ought to just come down and talk to Morey. Ask for some straight answers on their plans for me. So that's what I'm going to do. I've got my car packed and I'll be in Atlanta before the sun comes up in the morning. Did you know that Chuck and I started out together the same year with the Braves? Played together all the way from Rookie League to AAA at Richmond." Brett sighed and looked at his skipper. "And now Chuck Killian is the home run hitting star of the Atlanta Braves, and I'm on a bus to *Greenville.*"

"Well, good luck Brett. But be careful with Morey. He's a good man but real sharp, too. He didn't make himself one of the top general managers in the major leagues by making stupid decisions or saying things he shouldn't. But with Chuck's help, I'm pretty sure Morey will talk with you, hear you out."

"I hope so, Jimmy. I sure don't have anything to lose.

The bus rolled on into the dark Carolina night. Brett's thoughts turned to his mother. Elizabeth Davies had raised Brett alone, a single mom in the small southern town of Albemarle, North Carolina. It was not easy, but they did it. "We'll be fine Brett," she would always assure him, patting his blond hair gently, "as long as we stick together." And they did...and they were.

Brett never knew his father, so it was his mother who encouraged her son to play sports early on. She often reminded the youngster that he was named after her baseball hero, George Brett of the Kansas City Royals, and therefore "'had a lot to live up to.'" He excelled in football and basketball, but baseball was the sport Brett loved to play. His success as a young player, followed by his professional career in the Braves' organization, was a tremendous source of pride for her, as well as all their friends and family members back home. He would be returning to Albemarle soon, right after spending the weekend with Chuck and his family. He looked forward to starting his off- season job as a part-time teacher and coach at his old high school. Yet twenty-five years old and still living with his mother in the offseason weighed on his mind. *Where was the future Mrs. Brett Davies? My love life seems to be heading in the same direction as my baseball career...nowhere.*

Brett had gone out on plenty of dates, usually with a friend of one of his teammates' girlfriends, but nothing had ever clicked. *If I ever find the right girl, she better not be related to anyone playing baseball.*

Brett dozed off, awakening to the sound of the bus slowing down as it turned into the Greenville stadium parking lot. He grabbed his player's bag, found the rest of his equipment, and after some fast goodbyes to his teammates and coaches, settled into the front seat of his car to begin the drive to Chuck's house outside Atlanta. He popped a Nitty Gritty Dirt Band CD into the player and headed toward I-85 South.

The sun had not yet risen over the eastern horizon, and there were no lights on in the large two-story home when Brett pulled into the Killian driveway. He shut the engine off, got his bag, and walked around to the back of the stately home. He was relieved to find that Chuck's instructions as to where the key was hidden were indeed accurate. He unlocked the door and slipped upstairs to the guest bedroom.

This was not Brett's first visit to the home of the young Atlanta Braves star. He had stayed in the same room at Chuck's house two years earlier, but then he was a member of the major league team. A strong showing with the Braves' AAA club in Richmond (12 wins, 4 losses, and an ERA under 3.50) had earned Brett the opportunity to join Atlanta for the final month of the regular season. It was an exciting time as the Braves were in the middle of a heated pennant race with the Mets and Phillies. Despite the close standings, Brett was given an opportunity to pitch in several games, managing to win one while saving two others in relief. All the coaches and front office staff, including Morey, spoke to him before he left for home after the season, assuring Brett they had big plans for him to make the next step to the majors. Of course, those plans went away when he hurt his shoulder the following spring. Brett lay down on the bed as the troubling memories filled his head. He was too tired to process them any further and drifted off to a quiet sleep.

The smell of coffee and sounds of children laughing woke him from his deep slumber. Glancing at his watch, he groaned as he saw the first digit began with a seven. With a sigh he turned back over, putting the pillow over his head to drown the noises. He was used to going to bed after midnight and sleeping till ten or eleven in the morning (the life of a ball player can have significant advantages), but something told him today was not going to be anything like that.

"Mommy, Mr. Brett is here!" Brett turned over in time to see the back of a little blond head racing out of his room.

"Sophie, that can't be you. Sophie is a little girl."

"I am Sophie, Mr. Brett," she pronounced as she returned from the hallway, "and I am not a little girl. I'm four years old."

Before Brett could continue the discussion, Sophie turned and ran back out of the room. "He's finally awake, Mommy."

A quiet voice responded from the kitchen, "Sophie, let Mr. Brett sleep and come down here, your breakfast is ready---and don't wake your Daddy either."

Brett smiled to himself. Chuck got lucky when he met Sarah. *Maybe I'll get lucky someday, too.* He closed his eyes and pulled the blanket up higher around him.

It seemed like he had been asleep only a few minutes when he heard a familiar voice call his name. "Brett, get up old man. We got things to do today."

Brett smiled and opened his eyes to see his friend (and major league baseball star) Chuck Killian standing at the foot of his bed.

"Chuck, you're an All Star, a big league hero, idolized by children and their parents throughout the world, well Atlanta anyway, featured on ESPN highlights...what are you doing up so early on a Saturday morning?"

Chuck smiled, "Nice to see you, too. And congrats on getting that save last night up in Asheville. There was actually a small write-up in the sports page. You still got it, don't ya?"

"Ah, he was a rookie, Chuck. We'd never faced each other before. Jose called the pitch perfectly, and I just snapped off my side-arm curve. By the time he was finished ducking, it was all over. The kid didn't have a chance against the wily veteran, Brett Davies." Brett laughed and sat up in bed, waving to a perceived throng of admiring fans.

Chuck nodded, "Man, I hated it when you threw me that pitch. And those were our inter-squad games in spring training--I even knew it was coming. Listen, take a shower and get ready," he ordered. "We've got a 2 p.m. game today and I need to get down to the park by noon at the latest."

"OK, but do you know if Money Bags Morey will be there? I need to find out where I stand with this organization."

"I assume you mean our esteemed general manager, William Morey. Yeah, he's in town, wants to get a good look at all the young prospects we've brought up. And since we're ten games up on New York with less than a month to go, it's a good time to do it. Skip wants to start resting some of us for the playoffs."

Brett looked at his friend and spoke quietly. "Chuck, I should be one of those players. They brought me up two years ago before I hurt my arm. Remember, I was twelve and four at Richmond. Heck, I know Greenville is just AA, but I had thirty-two saves and my ERA was below three. They know I can do the job. My arm shouldn't be an issue. So, what gives?"

"I don't know old man." Chuck smiled and added slyly, "Maybe it's because they want to look at their *young* prospects."

"Thanks a lot, friend. Tell Sarah I'll be down in fifteen minutes."

"Good. She's been looking forward to your visit. And she's still trying to find you a soul mate, but so far, no luck. Says she can't find anyone good enough for you. Can you imagine that?"

"Well, tell her to keep looking."

"You tell her. Hurry up."

Brett showered, dressed, and walked down the winding stairs to the warm inviting kitchen of the Killian home. Sarah welcomed Brett with a big hug as soon as he entered the room.

"Hey, don't forget who you're married to," Chuck protested as he looked up from the sports page.

Sarah smiled at Brett, "And he better not forget either, right Brett?"

"That would definitely be my advice, Mrs. Killian."

"About time you got up, Mr. Brett." Brett quickly spun around and scooped Sophie up in the air before she could run away again. He twirled her around the room as she giggled excitedly. "Now here's my girl. Did you miss me?"

"Of course not," she sniffed. "I have lots of friends." The three adults laughed as Brett set Sophie down on the floor. She was up quickly and on to her next adventure.

"She doesn't stop, does she?" Brett looked at Sophie's parents only to receive two long sighs in reply to his question. "Where's Jimmy?" he asked.

"Oh, he's upstairs," Sarah responded. "I've got to get him to soccer practice in thirty minutes. Soccer Mom, that's me."

"Soccer?" Brett looked over at Chuck, but all he got in return was a shrug. "He likes it and he's pretty good, too. He played baseball this summer, and he's looking forward to basketball starting in a few months."

Sarah chipped in, "As long as he keeps his grades up, he can play. We don't push him any one direction."

"Not even baseball?"

"Nope, not even baseball," Sarah looked over at her husband and gave a knowing glance.

"She's the boss, old man."

As soon as Brett sat down at the big oak breakfast table, he realized he hadn't eaten anything since the previous afternoon. Sarah fixed that problem and Brett was soon feasting on a hot breakfast of bacon, eggs, grits, and biscuits. Brett took a sip of coffee and looked across the table at Chuck. "Man, if I ate like this every day, I'd be waddling out to the mound."

"It's not easy. We're a good team--she likes to cook, and I like to eat. Believe me, the club has a workout routine for me that guarantees I stay in playing shape. Got to maintain that All-American image, right honey?" Sarah laughed and threw her kitchen towel across the room, landing squarely on Chuck's head. Brett smiled to himself. *If only his fans could see the big league star at home.*

The Saturday morning ride into Atlanta was a welcome relief from the normal Monday through Friday traffic jams. Chuck turned the radio dial onto the local sports station to catch the last-minute updates on players and teams. There was little baseball news this morning. It was obvious that the two announcers were happy that college football would be starting soon.

"I wouldn't worry about Morey. Just say what you feel...get it out there and discuss it man to man. Heck, it's not like they can send you down to Greenville. You were already there." Chuck laughed at his own unique brand of humor but stopped when he saw the worried frown on Brett's face. He turned serious. "Listen Brett, I've heard them say plenty of good things about you this year when they were talking about Greenville. But there's still a question about your arm, even though the surgery was a success. How long has it been?"

Brett thought a moment before answering. He could still remember when it happened, a cool night for a spring training game in Orlando. Brett had been pitching well, but there wasn't a spot for him on the Atlanta roster. "Hang in there," they told him. "We'll be bringing you up the first chance we get."

He was up and down in the bullpen a lot that night.

"Get loose...sit down...warm up again...not yet...Brett you're in."

He remembered his arm feeling different, a little tight in the shoulder, but he was confident it would loosen up once he got in the game. There were runners on first and second, and he needed a ground-ball double play to get out of the inning. He kept the ball low, but his fastball missed the plate. Then on his second pitch he reached back to snap off an overhand curve. That was when his rotator cuff tore.

The rehab was long and painful. Surgery was bad enough, but the physical therapy pushed him to a level he had never experienced before. Brett worked hard, but progress was slow. He missed the entire season and had just begun to toss a baseball again in the off-season when it was time for spring training to begin. The trainers and coaches wanted to bring him along slowly. After all the teams headed north, he stayed in Florida a few extra weeks and began to throw stronger, eventually mixing in a few curveballs that further tested the repair work done on his damaged right shoulder. On the surface he appeared to be returning to his old form, but Brett knew differently. He could tell that his fastball didn't have the accustomed zip, or his curve the snap. His pitching coach encouraged him to work on a change up for a third pitch.

"You're not going to blow it by them right away, Brett my boy. Use your head, vary the location and speed, and keep 'em off balance. You'll be fine." *But fine for what?*

"I guess it's been eighteen months. Blew it out in March a year ago and missed the whole season. I didn't even try to throw a ball till last October." He was silent again. Chuck didn't say anything, his eyes straight ahead on the road as the Atlanta skyline appeared in the distance. The only sound came from the sport station DJs who were talking excitedly about Georgia Bulldogs football.

Brett broke the silence. "You know I never thought this would happen to me. Maybe get old and start losing some velocity or something, but to break down like that before I'm even thirty--I've never had an arm injury, or even a sore arm. Heck, it was just two years ago they called me up and you and I were driving into the games together. Then less than a year later..." his voice trailed off.

Finally, Chuck spoke up again. "Just tell them what you feel. But listen good, too. Who knows what plans they may have for you, or me for that matter?"

Just then Brett spotted a billboard as Chuck turned onto the entrance leading to the stadium. There, bigger than life, was Chuck Killian in his Braves uniform poised at the plate for the next pitch. "Get a hit for Special Olympics," the billboard read. The Atlanta Braves were donating a portion of this Labor Day weekend's gate receipts to the charity. There would be specially marked buckets for individual donations inside the stadium. Chuck wasn't just a major league star. In less than three years he had become a team leader and spokesman.

"I wouldn't be worrying about you," Brett laughed as Chuck pulled the car into the players' parking lot. "Old Money Bags Morey would never spring for the dollars it would take to change all your billboards."

3

OLD FRIENDS/NEW OPPORTUNITIES?

They got out of the car and, with Brett a few steps behind, Chuck strode quickly and confidently toward the entrance marked "Team Personnel Only." He was greeted with a big smile and slap on the back by the clubhouse attendant, Petey Jenkins, who was manning the door. Petey was an institution with the Braves organization, joining them as a lowly clubhouse boy when they first moved to Atlanta back in the 1960s. He swore to never retire, often saying he would much prefer to just die on the job.

"We're going to come in here one day, open the door, and find you lying on the floor, Petey. Dead as a doornail," Chuck joked.

"Yeah, but I'll be the one with a smile on my face," Petey growled. "You're back already, aren't you Chuck? Didn't you just leave here a few hours ago?"

"Less than twelve hours, Petey, my man. Hey, say hello to an old friend of yours." Petey looked over Chuck's shoulder and spotted Brett standing a few feet behind.

"*Brett Davies*. How you doing? Man, I haven't seen you in..."

"Two years to be exact Petey." Brett would never forget.

"Yeah, I guess that would be right. I heard about your shoulder and surgery and everything. Real tough break. But hey, I didn't know they had called you up. Your arm must be doing great."

"They didn't call me up, Petey. I'm just here visiting." There was a brief awkward silence. Chuck had already gone ahead to the team locker room. "I spent this year in AA up at Greenville. Did pretty good for missing one whole season. Chuck invited me to spend a couple days with him and his family, take in some games. Plus, I need to talk to Morey and find out what plans they have for me for next year.

"You're in luck, Brett," Petey whispered. He leaned closer to Brett as if he had the biggest secret in the world to share, and Brett was the lucky recipient. "Old Man Morey is in a pretty good mood. We're ten games up in the division with less than a month to go. So far everyone is staying pretty healthy. We're looking real strong right now." He looked around again to make sure no one was listening. "I hope we get the Yankees again in the Series, Brett. Those lucky sons of a guns got all the money and all the players. *It ain't fair.*"

Brett just smiled, fist bumping Petey, as he walked toward the clubhouse entrance. Grabbing the doorknob, he hesitated. Brett could hear the sweet mixture of laughter and music coming from inside. It was the sound of winners, a happy clubhouse. One he was once part of, but for a very brief time. A lot of his teammates from then were still on this year's Braves team. The next steps were going to be tough. Brett took a deep breath, opened the door and walked into the locker room. It only took a few seconds before it started.

From the far side of the room a voice boomed out, "*Guys, the new clubhouse boy is here. Wait a minute; he's too old to be a clubhouse boy.*"

A quick response...Brett thought he knew the voice but couldn't see the face. "*That's right; he must be here to pick up the laundry.*"

"Naw, that ain't it," drawled Cuban slugger, Manny Dominguez. "Laundry already been picked up."

"You know he looks familiar," said another voice from somewhere near the trainer's room. "I used to know someone that looked a lot like that guy--only younger."

Brett took it all in and smiled sheepishly. It hadn't taken Chuck long to spread the word. Other voices rang out.

"Hey, that's Brett Davies! Brett, how the heck are you? Where you been? Greenville? Maybe that's why you look so old and mangy!"

"... and his clothes don't fit either," the Braves star pitcher, Denny Stephenson chimed in. "Brett, this is the big leagues, right? We don't wear blue jeans up here. Gotta maintain that professional image, OK?"

Brett spoke for the first time.

"Gee, I'm sorry guys, but with my measly minor league salary this is all I could afford. I figured I could come back here and get a loan from some of my big league friends. Maybe then I could afford to go out and buy some proper threads"

With that a big roar of laughter erupted. The members of the division-leading, and confident-that-they-would-soon be World Series champions, Atlanta Braves crowded around Brett. He was hugged, picked up, slapped on the back, and punched in the ribs (all at the same time), while others made sure to mess his hair up. Brett loved it.

"Great to see you, Brett." It was Danny Allen, the Braves second baseman. "How's your shoulder? I hear you had a pretty good season in Greenville."

"Man, Danny, I didn't know you guys kept up with us minor league jocks."

"Not all of 'em Brett. Just a chosen few. Chuck was good about keeping us up to date on your rehab last year, and they print out all the minor league stats each week. Put them up on the bulletin board over there so we know who's trying to take our jobs." Danny laughed, then asked quietly, "You back 100%?"

"Almost, Danny, almost. I might have to work on my off-speed stuff more. It's been kind of hard to blow it by them, but I'm getting there."

"That's great, Brett. Hang in there and enjoy the games this weekend. It's good to see you."

Brett talked to a few more of his old teammates. The conversations were similar. He particularly appreciated the comments from the veteran Stephenson who had been an All Star pitcher for several years.

"You know Brett, same thing happened to me eight years ago. I was only twenty- seven and the daggone rotator cuff just snapped. No warning, no nothing. Physical therapy about killed me. I think that was worse than the operation, but you gotta do it." Brett smiled grimly, nodding in agreement as Denny continued.

"I sat out a year, just like you did, then went back to AAA for a few months to 'reinvent' myself. No more raring back and firing 90 mph fastballs past everyone. No sir, I had to become a pitcher, changing speeds, moving the ball around, studying the hitters more, make them hit your pitch. All that stuff I had been told for years and should have been doing but didn't have to--until I got hurt. Then, of course, I didn't have a choice." Denny laughed, "Brett, I'm thirty-five now, and those days seem long ago. I feel stronger than ever, too. I think pitching smarter is easier on my arm. It's going to give me a few more seasons. Much better than if I was still trying to strike everyone out. Same thing can happen to you."

Brett listened attentively and thanked the star pitcher for his encouragement. *Maybe I can do the same thing.* Of course, Denny had been an All-Star pitcher before his injury while Brett had only pitched in a handful of major league games. Still, you never know.

Brett walked over to Chuck's locker and sat down. Chuck already had his uniform pants and batting practice shirt on. He was just starting to lace up his spikes. "Thanks for providing the warm introduction, Chuck."

"No problem old man...just be glad these guys are your friends and not your enemies. Hey, I talked to Morey. Told him you were in town this weekend, and that you wanted to see him."

Brett was startled. He had half hoped to just walk in unannounced and catch Morey unprepared, maybe get a more truthful answer than some scripted comments about the need to " 'keep working hard and let's see what next year brings.'"

"Thanks a lot. What'd he say?"

"Nothing much. I told him you were going to be spending a few days with Sarah and me and the kids. He said he wanted to talk to you, too. So that sounded good to me."

"OK, should I go up there now?"

"Yeah, I would. Things will start getting hectic the closer we get to game time. Labor Day weekend, big crowds, plus the Special Olympics promotion, all that stuff. Oh, and I think we're going to be playing a baseball game, too." Chuck finished lacing up his spikes, stood up and took an envelope off the top shelf of his locker. "Here's your tickets for the games this weekend. I also put one in for Monday, but I know you said you would probably be heading home to Albemarle that day."

"Thanks, Chuck." Brett opened the envelope and checked the seat locations...lower level, first base side about fifteen rows up behind the Braves dugout. "Good seats, too."

"Yeah, you'll be sitting next to Sarah and the kids. You've got the extra family member ticket."

"Great, up there in the family section with all the wives and kids. I'll be the only semi-adult male in the whole area. It should be very entertaining."

Chuck smiled. "Hey old man, don't complain. Some of those wives have sisters, cousins, and girlfriends. The future Mrs. Davies might be getting to her seat right now as we speak."

Brett laughed. "I doubt it Chuck, but we'll see."

The rest of the Braves players were filing out of the locker room and heading for the field to start warming up. Brett walked down the long hallway toward the dugout with Chuck, Danny, and several others. He wished them all good luck in the game and turned down another aisle toward the elevator that would take him to the Braves executive offices. He looked back one last time at the sunshine filtered through the rear entrance to the field. Chuck and the others had disappeared. A low murmur came from the grandstands. The early arriving fans were greeting their beloved team as the players trotted out onto the sundrenched field. Brett was less than one hundred feet from the Major League world, but it felt like a hundred miles.

Stepping off the elevator, Brett was immediately reminded of the security issues from 9-11 that had made access to the Braves offices more regimented. Since he didn't have an ID card to swipe through the reader, he pushed the intercom button. A pleasant voice immediately answered, "May I help you?"

"Yes, I'm Brett Davies, here to see Mr. Morey."

"Oh yes, Brett. Mr. Morey said he thought you would be here this morning."

The buzzer sounded, Brett opened the door, and walked into the lobby of the Atlanta Braves executive offices. The paneled walls, soft light, and plush carpet made him feel like he was in some law office or banker's waiting room, but Braves' pennants and memorabilia throughout the room left no doubt as to where you were. The walls were lined with pictures of Braves teams and past and present heroes. Not surprisingly, a picture of Chuck Killian (completing, no doubt, another home run swing) was shown in a prominent display.

Sally Logan, executive assistant for the front office, greeted him. She was an attractive brunette, and today was totally decked out in full Braves gear, sporting a team t-shirt and hat, with matching earrings. There was no doubt that Sally was getting ready for a big day of Atlanta Braves baseball.

"Hi Brett, I met you a couple years ago when you were here to finish the season with us," she said. "How are you? I was so sorry to hear you hurt your arm. I understand things went really well for you in Greenville this year. I bet you'll be back with us in no time. Are you staying for the games this weekend?"

Brett smiled and shook Sally's hand. He dimly remembered meeting her. *Right now it seems like a lot longer than two years has gone by.* "Thanks Sally. Yes, I think my shoulder is coming around just fine. I'm looking forward to watching a couple games. Staying with Chuck and Sarah this weekend."

"Well that's great. I told Mr. Morey you were here. His office is down the hall, second door on the right so go on in, he's expecting you."

Brett walked nervously down the hallway, his heart pounding.

He stopped at the entrance to the GM's office. Baseball executive William Morey was on the phone talking excitedly to some lucky listener (Brett figured it was one of the Braves scouts) about an outfield prospect in the Cubs organization.

"I'm telling you Sam, the kid's going to be really good. I don't think the Cubbies know it or appreciate what they've got. He's only nineteen, good bat, good field, strong arm, all the tools. He's kind of skinny now, but he'll fill out. I want you to do some snooping around and see what the Cubs need. They're only two games back in the Central so you know they're looking for some extra help in the pennant race. Maybe we can give them one of our older vets, get someone that can help us in return and," Morey paused to make sure he had his listener's full attention, "at the last minute we get them to throw the kid in as part of the deal. *They won't even know what happened.*"

Brett smiled to himself. So this is how he does it. He had heard enough stories on how Morey worked the phone lines, gathering needed information to put another one of his magical deals together. The GM was famous for keeping the Braves balanced with veteran players and rising talent...and all the deals were at a salary level the team owners could afford. Two "Major League Baseball Executive of the Year" awards were prominently displayed so a visitor entering the room could not miss them. Other league officials were unanimous in their admiration of William Morey as the architect behind the Braves' success year after year.

Morey realized Brett was standing in the doorway and motioned for him to come in. With the phone conversation finished, he stood up from behind his desk and grabbed Brett's hand. "Great to see you, Brett. How are you doing?"

Brett was shocked. In his eleven years in the Braves organization, the only times he had ever talked to Morey were usually about contracts and money. Definitely not a pleasant experience for either of them. The GM seemed genuinely glad to see him. Of course, like Petey said, it didn't hurt that the team held a commanding lead in the pennant race as the season was winding down.

"I'm doing fine, Mr. Morey. We had a good year in Greenville. It was nice to be part of a team again after my year off."

"Yes, yes. The injury, rehab, all that. I've been keeping up with you, Brett." He smiled and winked, "That's my job you know."

Brett nodded and gave the GM a weak smile. He had never seen this side of one of baseball's leading executives.

Morey continued, "Brett, I apologize but we're not going to have much time to talk. Lots of stuff going on today--on the field and off--that I must attend to." He paused, "Chuck said you wanted to see me, so here we are. What's on your mind--or maybe I can make an educated guess?"

Brett's mind was racing. He was beginning to feel lightheaded. *Stay calm, remember what Chuck said, tell him how you feel, what you want to know. "Just don't blurt it out, old man, or throw up on anything either."* Brett took a deep breath. He was only going to get one chance at this.

"Yes sir, I'm sure you probably could. I really appreciate your taking the time to see me today." He hesitated and decided to dive right in. "Mr. Morey, I'm at a point in my career where I need your honest opinion as to where I stand with the Braves organization. Two years ago, I was up here in September as a player and pitched pretty well for the club."

"I remember," Morey assured him. Brett continued. He was on a roll now.

"Then, as you know, I hurt my shoulder, had surgery and went through the long rehab which caused me to miss all of last year." He looked for a reaction, but Morey said nothing. "Now, after missing that whole year I just finished up what I feel was a successful season in Greenville. I think I'm back, my arm is getting stronger, and I'm learning to pitch smarter, too, just like Denny Stephenson has done." Brett didn't think it would hurt to remind Morey that his star pitcher had come back from the same injury. He took another deep breath. "Mr. Morey, I just need to know what the Braves feel my opportunities are for the future." Brett stopped, looking intently at the GM. He had said what he wanted. *It was time to shut up and listen.*

Morey smiled and reached for a folder on the credenza behind his desk. Brett realized that the windows in the office gave the general manager a clear view of the Braves diamond.

"I've got one of these for each of our boys, Brett." He held the folder out and Brett could see his name neatly typed on the index tab. "Let's see what we've got here. Now understand, I don't have the end-of-season reports yet, but I do get enough information throughout the season, from the managers and scouts, that I have a pretty good file on each player."

Morey studied the notes inside Brett's folder for a few long moments before continuing. "Well, the quick report, and as I've said that's all I have time for today, is that we've got good news and bad news."

Brett was listening. *Where's this going?* "Your statistics were very good, ERA, saves, etc. especially considering you were coming back after missing the entire previous season. Let's see, you pitched mostly in relief, one to three innings at a time. I like the low number of walks and the stats indicate most of the balls hit off you were on the ground. Means you were keeping the ball low, getting double plays. That's what we need in our relief pitchers, no walks, and if you make a mistake, at least keep it down so they can't drive the ball out of the park."

"On the other hand, the scouts say you've lost a lot of your speed. You were throwing in the low nineties before your injury, but now you're only mid-eighties. That's a big drop. And, of course, you did all this in Greenville. That might not be far in mileage from Atlanta, but it's a long way from the big leagues."

Brett started to respond, but Morey held his hand up indicating he should remain quiet. The GM paused for a few moments glancing over the notes in Brett's folder again. Brett had no way of knowing that Morey had decided not to mention the trainer's reports on the long hours Brett struggled to be ready to pitch just a few innings at a time. *Alternating ice and heat treatments on the shoulder, stretching, massage, weights...*and some days the trainer reported to the manager, unknown to Brett, *it would probably be better to not pitch him today.*

"Brett, here's what I think. You're still in the mix; you'll be playing somewhere next year. In fact, depending on all the other reports, I may be able to invite you to our major league camp in February. You'd get your opportunity to show us what you can do down there." Brett's heart jumped. He nodded to Morey and leaned forward in his chair. *Big league spring training camp.* That would be his big chance to go against all the other clubs' best prospects and prove he still has what it takes to play at the major league level.

Morey continued, "But you know, Brett, it's still obvious to us that you're a long way from being 100% back to where you were before you got hurt. We'll give you the opportunity. Maybe you'll get stronger or change your style and be successful like Denny. Who knows what will happen? Ultimately that's not up to me; it's only up to the young man sitting across my desk to show us what he can do."

Morey stood up and Brett followed. "Sorry, Brett, but I have to cut this short. We'll be in touch this winter about your contract. You'll also get info about spring training, when and where, all that stuff."

They shook hands. Brett knew it was time to leave. He remembered to thank the Braves executive and turned to head out the door. Before reaching the hallway, he heard the GM's voice.

"You know Brett, there is one more thing you need to think about."

Brett turned around, puzzled but anxious to hear what Morey had to say.

"We've been watching your style and mannerisms over the years, son. We can tell you're a student of the game. Don't you coach and teach in the off-season at your high school back home?"

Brett nodded but said nothing.

"This past season your coaches, both Graham and Simonetti, have mentioned several times how you were working with our young guys out in the bullpen. It was obvious they were listening to you and respected what you had to say. We could see the results of all you were doing when they went out to pitch. That's a wonderful skill, something you must have been born with. It's also something for you to think about real hard. You have a gift for teaching and coaching. The Braves' organization needs coaches and managers with that gift to ensure our future success. You could be one of them Brett-- maybe sooner rather than later." Morey sat down and picked up the phone to make another call.

Brett walked out of Morey's office, his mind racing. One minute Morey is talking about him going to spring training with the big club, and the next he's saying he could be a coach in the Braves organization. He shook his head and headed out of the office for the elevator. *Well, I guess I at least have some opportunities.... but which ones?* He pushed the elevator button and awaited the ride that would take him down to the stadium and back into the world of major league baseball.

4

GOING HOME

B rett knew the drive from Chuck's suburban Atlanta home to the Davies' residence in Albemarle, North Carolina would take him about seven hours...six if he pushed it. He had called his mother before leaving and let her know he would "definitely be home in time for dinner." This pleased her immensely, as Elizabeth Davies loved nothing more than preparing a big home-cooked meal for her only son.

The Labor Day morning traffic was light, and Brett figured most people were probably squeezing as much holiday out of the weekend as they could. He welcomed the unusual emptiness of the highway and soon found himself exiting the Atlanta beltway and merging onto I-85 heading north for Charlotte. Going home felt good.

Brett set the cruise control on seventy and put a Garth Brooks CD into the car's stereo system. A lot had happened in Atlanta during the two short days he was there. He smiled thinking about Chuck, Sarah, and the kids. Leaving them was tough, even for Sophie who, after reminding Brett (once again) that "she had lots of friends," jumped into his arms for a final swing around the room.

"Please come back soon, Mr. Brett. I hope you can play a baseball game with my Daddy when you do." Everyone laughed at the innocent wisdom of Sophie's remarks. To the little girl, baseball was only a game to have fun playing, but to Chuck Killian and Brett Davies it would always be much more.

Chuck grabbed Brett's arm firmly. "You mind what my little girl said, old man. I'll see you in spring training. *Let's count on it.*"

"I hope you're right, Chuck. Morey told me it was a possibility. He sure didn't have to say anything like that to me."

Sarah gave Brett a big hug. "Say hello to your mother for us, Brett. She's a wonderful woman."

"Well she put up with me for almost twenty-six years. Heck, I'm almost thirty and still living at home."

They all laughed one more time and walked out of the house together to Brett's car. Chuck and Sarah knew his mother well. They had insisted Mrs. Davies stay with them two years ago when she came to Atlanta to watch her son's debut with the Braves. She thoroughly enjoyed her visit to the big city, especially since she had never attended a major league game before. She was almost overwhelmed by the experience, and it was comforting to sit with Sarah and the children. Elizabeth Davies simply could not believe that her Brett was actually playing in the beautiful Atlanta stadium.

Brett was fairly certain someone clued in Manager Schulz that his mother was going to be there because that weekend he got to pitch in two of the three games she saw. When she left Sunday evening to return to Albemarle, Sarah had assured her, "Don't you worry, Mrs. Davies, we'll take good care of your son. And I'm going to keep looking till I find the right special someone for him. *Someone just as good as you, if that's possible.*"

Brett had heard that last part and just shrugged his shoulders, as his mother pointed her finger at him. "You do that, Sarah. Lord knows the boy needs someone to take care of him. I can't do it all the time anymore."

Brett smiled at the memory as his thoughts shifted back to baseball and the "opportunities" Morey had laid out to him. Nothing more was said, but after the Braves' Saturday game, pitching coach, Mack Simpson, approached Brett as he was talking to some of the players in the locker room.

"How you doing, Brett? "

"Fine Coach. It's been a lot of fun to be up here these past couple days."

"Well, we were all thinking you might like to throw some BP for us before the game tomorrow. What do you think?"

Brett could still feel the emotions that ran through him as he stepped out of the dugout and onto the field wearing his Atlanta Braves uniform. Walking out to the mound everything seemed sharper and brighter. It was still more than two hours before the

8 p.m. start of the ESPN Sunday night game, but the Braves players were already in rare form. Brett enjoyed being in the middle of the friendly chatter and good-natured ribbing that was going on all around him. While some of it was directed at him, the Braves had plenty left over for each other. "Hey Brett, what you doing out there? You need help getting up on the mound? Watch out guys, we got some AA heat throwing batting practice tonight."

Brett pitched smoothly, laying the ball in for the hitters to get their swings. His arm and shoulder felt surprisingly good. *Probably the adrenaline.* He looked up above home plate to where he thought the Braves executive offices were located. He couldn't be sure, was that Morey looking down from his office...or was that even his office?

Brett was scheduled to throw for twenty minutes, which would be enough for about five or six Braves batters before the next pitcher took over. He was working up a good sweat on the hot September afternoon, enjoying everything about being out on a major league mound again...even if it was only practice. Chuck was going to be his last batter, so he carefully laid the ball in right where he knew his friend liked it. The Braves slugger responded with several titanic shots that sailed high over the outfield wall deep into the bleachers. The fans that had arrived early to watch batting practice cheered and clapped their hands in delight with each swing.

Suddenly Chuck stepped out of the batter's box and pointed his bat at Brett.

"All right, old man, let's see what you got." Chuck tapped his bat on home plate for emphasis as Brett tried to hold back his surprise at the challenge. He looked around and noticed that several Braves players had stopped what they were doing and were quickly gathering around the batting cage to see what would happen next.

"OK, Chuck. You want to get embarrassed by a minor league relief pitcher with a rebuilt shoulder, be my guest." Brett looked in at his catcher, Billy Kowalski. "One fastball, two curve, three for the change. OK, Billy?" Kowalski nodded and crouched back down behind home plate. By now most of the Braves coaching staff had joined the crowd around the cage and were watching with interest as the scene played out.

Brett decided his first pitch would be a fastball, but *nothing too good.* He knew from past experience how hard it was to throw a pitch past Chuck Killian. He took his windup and at the last second decided to drop down sidearm. He aimed for the inside half of the plate and released the ball with as much backspin as he could muster. To his relief the ball did what it was supposed to. Chuck had started his swing, but as the ball reached home plate, it dove in on his hands and he could only foul the pitch off down the third base line.

The reaction from behind the cage was immediate. *"Strike one,"* a Braves player shouted. The banter from the players moved back and forth. Loud encouragement for Brett while Chuck was "gently reminded" that he was a "big league star" and not to embarrass himself...or the Atlanta Braves.

Billy signaled for another fastball, but Brett shook him off. He was waiting for the change up, and when Billy flashed three fingers down, Brett nodded his head in agreement. *Give him the big motion, take something off of it, and hope the ball dies before it gets to home plate. Gotta keep it low.*

Brett took his windup, exaggerating the motion slightly and wheeled toward home plate, squeezing the ball in the back of his hand so it would slip slowly out of his grip as he released it. Chuck had heard all his teammates talk and was overanxious. He was way out in front of the pitch and swung a split-second too soon as the change up dropped below his knees. A low murmur swept through the watching players and coaches as Chuck could only slap the ball into the ground behind the plate.

"*Strike two.*" The murmur had turned to a low roar.

"Come on, Brett!"

"Set him down, Davies!"

"You can do it...finish the big star off!"

And for Chuck there was no let up.

"One more strike, Mr. Killian, and Morey's gonna talk to you about a new contract...in AA!"

"What's the matter, Chuck? This guy just got his shoulder cut on. He got your number?"

Brett took a deep breath and contemplated his next pitch. *The problem is that Chuck and I have played together so much we know exactly our strengths and weaknesses. There's no way I can surprise him.*

Normally Brett's tendency would be to go to his favorite strike out pitch, the big sidearm curve. But Chuck would know that and be looking for it. Brett shook his head, the shouts of the Braves players echoing in his ears. He peered in at the plate to get Billy's sign as Chuck readied himself in the batter's box. Suddenly a new thought popped into his head. *What if Chuck knows what I know, and he starts thinking about what I'm thinking? He'll think that I think he's thinking I'm going with the curve. He'll be guessing fastball.* Brett paused to steady himself. *These mind games can get to you.*

Brett made his decision. He shook Billy's signals off several times, making him call for the curve a second time. *That should keep Chuck thinking . . . at least I hope it does.* Brett touched the back of his neck with his pitching fingers and got just enough moisture to get a good grip on the ball. The batting cage crowd was quiet now as they watched Brett start his windup. He pushed off the rubber and, as he had done so many times before, stepped toward the third base line and flung the ball across his body with a big snap of his wrist.

The ball headed for the inside part of the plate and Chuck started to open his stride so he could pull the "fastball" down the left field line. It was then he realized he had guessed wrong. The ball darted across the plate cutting the outside part of the strike zone before landing in Kowalski's mitt. Hopelessly out of position, unable to reach that part of the plate, Chuck could only stand there and watch the ball sail by.

Brett looked in at Chuck. "Strike three?"

"Strike three, old man. You got me again."

By now all the Braves players were in an uproar. Brett walked triumphantly off the mound, feeling tired yet pleased with his performance. He was not sure what to think about what had just happened, but he gratefully accepted the congratulations and back slapping from the major leaguers and smiled at the good-natured ribbing Chuck was forced to endure. He went into the dugout and grabbed a towel to wipe the sweat off his face. Plopping onto the bench, he felt exhausted. Looking up, he saw Chuck walk over to him.

"You still got it, Brett. Don't let anyone tell you different. I am going to make sure that Morey invites you to spring training with us."

"Thanks, Chuck. But you didn't have to do that."

"Do what?"

"You know. Challenging me to pitch to you, acting like you got fooled. I couldn't have faked you out that much."

"Think what you want. All I know is what I saw and so do the rest of our guys, including Morey and the coaches."

"Morey was watching?"

"Let me give you a big hint, Brett. Morey sees everything."

The trip passed quickly as Brett continued to review his season and all the possibilities for the coming year. Before he knew it, he had reached the Charlotte area and was exiting the I-485 beltway onto NC Highway 27, Albemarle Road. Forty-five minutes later he pulled into the driveway of the Davies family home on Cannon Street. He honked the horn once, and in a matter of seconds Elizabeth Davies came out onto the front porch waving happily, relieved at the safe arrival of her only child.

Mrs. Davies was an attractive energetic woman with just a few streaks of gray starting to show through her short blond hair. She loved telling anyone listening that she was "still 39 and planned to stay that way for a long time." For the most part, her friends and family had no reason to doubt her. She was only eighteen years old when Brett was born, and she took on the responsibility of raising him by herself. Brett had never known his father, but monthly child support checks came in on a regular basis and helped the little family pay their bills. His mother did not talk about Brett's dad. As he grew up, he had learned to ask few questions about the absent parent in his life.

It was a tough busy life for the young Davies family. Brett and his mother often joked later that they grew up together, and in many ways it was true. They were mother and son, but they were also best friends. She was always there for him as the boy grew into a young man, an honor student, and a star on every sports team he played on. She had plenty of opportunities to date, even invited to join the church singles club, but she was not interested. Her concentration was on raising her son.

Now that Brett was grown and away from home most of the year, her life had simplified a great deal. She still enjoyed working as a secretary at the law office of Sharpe and Patterson, a position she had held almost thirty years. She was proud that she had come a long way from the scared, pregnant teenager that sat in Mr. Patterson's office asking for a job. The law firm kept her busy during the week and, combined with her volunteer work at the Albemarle United Methodist Church, she was a busy and content woman. But the best times in her life were always those when Brett could get home for a brief visit during the season or now during the "off-season" when he would be with her until it was time to go back to baseball in the spring.

Brett embraced his mother with a big hug, and then picked her up, swinging her once around despite her delighted protests that the neighbors would see them. Finally, he set her down.

"You must be famished, Brett. Get your things and let's get inside. Dinner's waiting."

Brett smiled. He had learned long ago his mother's first rule of Southern hospitality started with food. "That sounds good, Mom. I haven't had much to eat since breakfast at Chuck's, and that was a long time ago."

"Well, grab your things and come on in. I've made sure everyone knows you're home. Oh, Mr. Harland at the high school wants you to come in tomorrow so they can review your schedule. He's looking forward to having you back. I think our teams could use some extra coaching, too...both on and off the field. Darnell needs your help," she added for emphasis, referring to Brett's childhood friend who was now his school's head football coach. High school sports were big time in the little town of Albemarle and that had not changed for Mrs. Davies, even after Brett had graduated.

"Wow, Mom," Brett protested. "The season just ended three days ago. Don't I at least get a week of R&R?"

Elizabeth Davies looked up at her son and smiled. "Somehow, I think you'll get rested up just fine. Spring training doesn't start till March, which gives you six months."

"Maybe less than that, Mom. They're talking about inviting me to the big club's training camp. I'd be going down to Florida in February if that happens."

Mrs. Davies gave Brett another hug and hung onto his arm as they turned to walk back into the house together. "Brett, that would be just wonderful."

5

BACK TO SCHOOL

Brett's alma mater, Stanly County High School, was built on the tallest hill in the town of Albemarle. On sunny days the view from the third floor windows allowed students and faculty a clear look across the county toward the tall bank buildings of Charlotte to the west and the ancient Uwharrie Mountains and Lake Badin to the east. The bell tower was the highest point on the school. Brett could recall climbing the winding narrow staircase of the tower vestibule with his senior teammates to ring the victory bell after defeating their archrivals, the Concord Cardinals.

Brett navigated his car up the winding tree-lined road leading to the school entrance and smiled as memories of victory bells and other athletic accomplishments came flooding back to him. While it was unique to have the school situated above the surrounding countryside, the only level playing fields for the football and baseball teams were a half mile back down the hill to the county park. Over the years the players of Stanly County became convinced that the daily one-mile round trip down and back up the hill for practices and games significantly helped their training program. In fact, all knew it was one of the major reasons for their success on the field.

Brett had called the school earlier that morning to let Principal Charles Harland know he was home and ready to get to work. Harland was in good spirits for a Monday. "That's great news, Brett," he said. Good to hear from you and have you back. Stop in to see me first when you get here, and we'll get you lined up where we need help most. I know for sure that Darnell will be real glad to see you."

"Yes sir, I'm ready to head out the door now. Be there in just a few minutes." Brett didn't think it necessary to tell the principal that his mother had already fed him breakfast and made a lunch for him to take to school. He hung up the phone just as Mrs. Davies handed him a large brown paper bag stuffed with enough food to last several meals. "You know, Mom, they do serve lunch at school."

"I know Brett, but these are just a few leftovers from dinner last night. Don't want them to go to waste."

Brett sighed and headed out the door. *At least she doesn't follow me to the bus anymore.*

Upon entering the school, Brett headed straight for the administrative area and knocked on the open door of the principal's office. He was greeted with a big smile and firm handshake from Harland, a short slightly graying man with wire-rimmed reading glasses perched on his nose. "Great to see you again, my boy. How are you doing? You're looking great. They must have increased the meal money again for you ball players." He laughed at his own joke and offered Brett a seat.

Brett had known Charles Harland for almost twenty years. It sometimes seemed that they had gone to school together but in different roles. As Brett had progressed from one grade to the other in the Stanly school system, so had the principal from teaching positions in elementary, middle and high schools to administrative duties that eventually led to his appointment three years ago as principal of the town's high school. Brett remembered him best as his favorite math teacher in high school. Harland had spent his entire career making Stanly County schools the best they could be, and he wasn't going to let a little budget crunch stop him now.

"Brett, your being here is a real boost for us," he said. "I don't know if you were aware of this, but we're understaffed again in the athletic department...darned state budgets...so your being with us on a part-time basis is excellent timing."

"Yes sir, Mom said things were tough...especially now with enrollment up and everything."

"Well it is what it is, so we just deal with it. They put a freeze on hiring more full-time employees, but" he paused and leaned closer to Brett across the desk, "they didn't say anything about part-time ball players waiting for spring training to start."

Brett nodded and smiled. "I guess that makes me qualified, especially with that fringe benefit package you don't have to pay me."

"Well that's not the only reason Brett, but it sure doesn't hurt the numbers, if you know what I mean."

"Fair enough. Where can I help you the most? I've really enjoyed working with all the guys on the teams of course the last few years. And I wouldn't mind doing some tutoring or substitute teaching in math and science if you need me there, too."

"That's exactly what we had in mind, Brett. Coach Motley is totally tied up with the football team right now, but his baseball players are anxious to get started with fall practice. You can get that going and also help Darnell in football. As far as your student tutoring, I'll pass the word out to the teachers that you're back and ready for assignments. Most of them already know you got home yesterday."

Brett grimaced. *Good ol' Mom.*

His next stop was to the athletic office of head football and baseball coach, and Brett's good friend, Darnell Motley. The coach was glad to see help had arrived.

"Man, oh man, Davies; it's about time you showed up. Where you been anyway? Oh, I know... playing a game of baseball no doubt." Darnell grabbed Brett's hand and held it tightly. Brett had made a mental note years ago to always shake hands firmly with his friend, but to let go quickly to avoid having his hand crushed. Motley was a big man at 6 feet 6 inches tall and probably tipping the scales at 250 pounds. As far as Brett could tell the former high school and college star was still in pretty good shape. The two had known each other since they were little kids playing in the town's recreation league, but it was not until they were in middle school that the two athletes were able to compete on the same team.

Darnell was two years older than Brett and his poise and natural ability made him an instant leader for the younger man to follow and emulate. Like Brett, Darnell played all three sports--football, basketball, and baseball; but where Brett's best moments came on the ball diamond, Motley became famous as the anchor of the state champion Albemarle Wildcats defensive line that allowed only two touchdowns their entire senior season. Brett was a sophomore that year and, when the Wildcats' starting quarterback went down with an injury, he was thrown in as the offensive leader of the team. The tough Wildcats defense, with Motley in charge, helped put their offense, with Brett at the controls, in good field position time after time. Darnell also played on the offensive line. He made sure there was no way his young friend was going to fail.

"Well, I guess I got here just in time, Mr. Coach Darnell Motley, Sir. Harland said you couldn't handle two teams at once for some reason; so once again, I must ride to your rescue and take care of fall baseball practice--maybe help the football team a little bit too, work with your quarterback some. I can't imagine a beat-up old lineman will be able to teach our QB's very much worthwhile."

Darnell gave Brett a long withering look before erupting in laughter. "You are absolutely right, Brett, my man. You are, oh so, absolutely right."

It did not take long for Brett to settle in at his old high school. Tutoring students in math and chemistry plus occasional duties as a substitute teacher filled his days. Then it was off to the practice fields where he would first get the baseball team started in its fall practice sessions before rushing over to the football field to help Darnell with the offensive squad of the Wildcats team.

This was Brett's third year at Stanly. Previous off-seasons had been devoted to getting his education degree from UNC-Charlotte. He was drafted by the Braves after his junior year, and it took three years going part-time in the off-season to complete his senior year. It was a lot of work, but he fulfilled the promise he made to his mother to complete his education when he opted to sign with the Braves. Of course the signing bonus offered by the team was also a big enticement. Brett used it to help his mother get a new car and do some much-needed remodeling on their family home. The topper of the deal, however, came when Mrs. Davies made Winston Carson, the Braves- veteran scout, agree to also pay for Brett's senior year tuition, "but only if he makes a B or better, of course," she explained, looking at Brett with a knowing smile.

Armed with his degree and teaching certificate, as well as his reputation as a member of the Atlanta Braves organization, Brett was welcomed with open arms by the teachers, coaches, and administrators at Stanly High. He was a different kind of teacher, of course, only being at the school for half the year before heading south to play baseball every March. There was no doubt that this uniqueness (and the aura of the Atlanta Braves) helped him relate well with the young students, especially the athletes who reminded Brett what it was like to be the "big man" of the high school team, complete with all the accompanying glory on the outside and nervousness on the inside. Nevertheless, he often found himself spending a lot of time with the self-proclaimed "geeks" or "nerds" of the school. As he helped them understand their math and science assignments, he learned to respect and appreciate their interests in art, music, drama, and other subjects Brett had never dreamed of experiencing on his own as a high school jock.

Friday Night Football was big time for the little town of Albemarle. The fans came out early to line the driveway as the marching band led the team down the hill to Wildcats stadium. The home team side of the field was always filled to overflowing regardless of the opponent with fans of all ages. There were parents, grandparents, other friends and relatives, plus former players and, of course, the young future stars who ran up, down, and under the stadium bleachers before (and sometimes after) the kickoff.

Darnell was only too glad to hand over the offensive play calling to his friend, the former star quarterback, so he could concentrate on the defensive strategy. They now stood together again on the sideline as they had done on so many long-ago fall Friday nights. It was easy for Brett to let his mind wander back to those days when the two teammates led Stanly High to victory after victory on that same football field. But Brett didn't daydream for long. There were games to be played...and won. The pressure was intense as the expectations for the team were high. The good folks of Albemarle expected their boys to win and every player on the team knew it. Brett could sense the anticipation mixed with excitement (and sometimes a little fear) as Darnell addressed them before every game.

"You young men know what to do. We've looked at film together...we've practiced our plays together...we've sweated and worked our tails off to be ready for tonight. Gentlemen, there are only so many Friday night football games that you will ever play in your lifetime. Let's make this game, this game tonight, one to remember, one to be proud of, one to tell your children and grandchildren about some day. *Let's do it.*"

With that Darnell clapped his hands and the players rushed forward around him, all shouting and cheering, placing a hand in the center of the growing circle. After a few moments, Motley motioned for silence and held his huge right hand high over his head, the fingers spread apart. All eyes were on their coach.

"Gentlemen, separate we will be weak and fail." Slowly he closed his fingers tightly into a fist. "Together we will stand strong and succeed." As one, all players raised their right hands, formed a fist, and thrust it into the circle together. *Tonight is our night. Let's go Wildcats...1, 2, 3, TEAM.!* Thus united, with a crescendo of noise, the Stanly Wildcats charged out of the locker room. As they burst through the banner under the goal posts, the marching band began playing the school fight song. The cheerleaders, students, parents, and other fans screamed out their love and affection for their Wildcats, urging and pleading with them to get another victory for Stanly High.

It was a scene Brett loved to remember and be a part of again every Friday night. And the team was successful, too. As the nights got crisper and colder, September turned to October, and the Wildcats finished the regular season with a record of eight wins and only one loss. They were peaking at the right time, ready for the North Carolina Division 2A High School playoffs. Brett and Darnell felt nothing could stop them. But very soon something totally unforeseen would.

6

TERRIBLE NEWS

B rett pulled his car into the teacher's parking lot the Monday morning after the football team's last regular season game. It was a new week and time to get ready for the playoffs. His mind was racing. There was a lot to do in the next four days. They had found out their opponent was from Alamance County, but Brett and Darnell knew nothing about them. *At least we seem to be in pretty good shape mentally and physically.* Brett was confident as he entered the school lobby and headed for his desk in the athletic department.

"Brett, we need you in Mr. Harland's office right away. It's urgent."

He turned around to see Assistant Principal Patty Matthews hurrying toward him. "Sure Patty, no problem. I'm sorry, was I supposed to be at a meeting...?"

Patty interrupted him, "No Brett, this just came up a few minutes ago. I'm not sure. It doesn't look good, it's terrible. I hope it isn't true."

"What are you talking about?"

"Just hurry, Brett."

He was perplexed now...and worried. Brett followed Patty back to the school administration area and was directed to a small meeting room next to Principal Harland's office. Upon entering he glanced around the room, trying to get a sense of what was going on. The first person Brett saw was Darnell. He was seated at the table with his head down, rubbing his huge hands over his forehead. It only took a few seconds to realize Patty was right-- it didn't look good. Harland was across the table from Darnell, speaking in a hushed tone to two other men. Brett didn't recognize the one fellow wearing a sport coat and appeared to be doing most of the talking. The other individual he did know. It was Albemarle police chief, Raymond Hightower.

Brett sat down next to Darnell and waited. The other men finished their conversation and took their seats across the table from the two coaches. Principal Harland spoke first. "Thank you for joining us, Brett." He paused for a moment, "You haven't missed much. Let me first introduce you to these gentlemen. On my right is Steve Berlinger. Steve is an executive with the North Carolina High School Athletic Association."

Brett nodded but didn't say anything. *NCHSAA, Patty was right, something really bad has happened.*

Harland continued, "This other gentleman..."

"That's OK, Charles," Brett interrupted. "All us Albemarle kids know Chief Hightower." The chief smiled at Brett and nodded. He had followed Brett's athletic career all through high school and now with the Braves. Like all the other Albemarle natives, he was proud of this young man who was born and raised in their town.

"Nice to meet you, Brett. You getting ready to join the Atlanta team this spring?"

Before Brett could reply, Berlinger cleared his throat and spoke. "Let's continue our meeting, shall we?" All eyes were now on the high school official. "Gentlemen, I'll bring you coaches up to date and come right to the point. Our North Carolina athletic office received evidence last week, which we since have been able to confirm, that one of the young men on your football team has been taking anabolic steroids to improve his performance."

For a brief moment Brett could not absorb what he had just heard. *Steroids?* He looked to his friend. "Darnell, what's going on?"

The coach looked up for the first time. His voice was soft and hoarse. "I don't know, Brett. I swear, I don't. This is the first I've heard of it too. They say it's Derek."

Derek Jones, the team's senior captain and All-State middle line-backer. He had already been offered scholarships several top college programs. Ohio State, North Carolina, Clemson...what *would happen now, if it is true?*

Berlinger continued, "You both should know that a tremendous amount of investigation in a relatively short time frame has been done prior to this meeting. We've checked and cross-checked our sources. Derek was getting the drugs from a doctor down in Florence. With the cooperation of our friends in the South Carolina law enforcement agencies, as well as our counterparts in the state athletic office, we have confirmed that Derek visited this doctor's office eight different times since last March--once a month."

"The South Carolina officials were doing their own investigation down there on this guy, Chief Hightower added. "When they confronted him last week, the doctor admitted to everything, trying to plea bargain, I suppose. He gave them names, places, times, prescriptions--the whole works. When they saw Derek's name on the list, they called my office."

"And then they called me, and I called the NCHSAA." Harland paused before continuing, "I apologize, but it was my decision not to tell you coaches at the time. This all just came down Thursday morning and had not been verified. Plus, you were getting ready to play a football game. Frankly, I was hoping it wasn't true." He stopped and looked at Darnell and Brett. "We decided to search Derek's locker this weekend. The chief and I found steroids in there, as well as unfilled prescriptions made out to Derek by the doctor."

Darnell continued to sit in his chair, not looking up. Brett had never seen his friend so despondent. *What can they do now? What will happen to Derek? What about the playoffs?* "Has anyone talked to Derek yet?"

"We've called his parents," Harland responded. "And Derek should be sitting outside in the waiting area by now. His folks will be here at nine." Everyone looked at their watch. "That's in ten minutes."

Darnell spoke to the North Carolina official. "If this is true, if Derek admits he did this, what will you do to my player? What will you do to my team?" His voice trailed off, almost like a cry for help. Everyone was looking at Berlinger for the answers.

"Well, the easy decision--and I only mean the decision, not the impact on the young man -- is that Derek will not be allowed to play any more football or any other sport for Stanly High. His career is finished." He hesitated and looked around the room. All the other men nodded. They knew that was the only choice the North Carolina office had.

"What about my team, the playoffs?"

"Well, that's going to take some discussion, and we'll have to do it fast. This is Monday, and the playoffs start on Friday. That's only four days away. Once the news gets out, the press will be going crazy. Keep in mind that there are these meetings going on right now in several other high schools in North and South Carolina. The doc was a busy man. The story of steroids mixed with high school football will, no doubt, be huge. We'll need to have a special meeting of the State athletic board of directors. My guess is it'll be tomorrow afternoon. I'll be getting back to the office later today and will call you, Charles, with the time you and Coach Motley will need to be there."

"We're going to Raleigh?" Darnell looked across the table at his principal.

"Yes." Berlinger confirmed. "It is very important that both of you attend this meeting to represent the interests of your school."

The meeting was interrupted by a knock on the door. Patty Matthews peeked in. "Derek and his parents are here. Should I have them come in?" Harland nodded and a few seconds later a bewildered Wayne and Cindy Jones entered the room followed by their only son.

Brett watched Derek walk in. The young athlete stared straight ahead, not acknowledging the presence of his coaches. Even though he played on the defense, Brett felt he knew the young star well. Besides tutoring Derek in math, he also was part of the weekly coaches and captains meeting held each Monday. Brett remembered thinking the linebacker had gained quite a bit of weight and muscle since he had last seen him the previous year but thought nothing more of it. Just a young man, eighteen years old, starting to fill out as an adult. He was a vocal leader on and off the field, but never any signs of steroid-induced rage, or other problems which Brett had always heard associated with the dangerous drugs.

Wayne Jones was a prominent banker in the small community and used to running his own meetings. "What's going on here, Harland?" he snapped. "Why have you called us down here?" Jones looked around the room at his son's coaches and the two other men. "And why on earth is the police chief here? Are you saying my boy's committed some kind of crime?" He was now looking directly at Berlinger, the only person in the room he didn't know.

Harland stood up and motioned for the family to take the three remaining chairs around the table. "No one's going to jail. Please sit down, Wayne. All of you, please sit down." Harland continued, determined to keep control of his meeting.

"Now Wayne, I need you to listen for a few minutes to what we have to say. I'll make sure you have plenty of time to have your questions answered. This is Mr. Steve Berlinger. He is an executive with the North Carolina High School Athletic Association."

Berlinger proceeded to lay out the entire story of the investigation on the South Carolina doctor. Brett thought he saw Derek's face flinch for just a moment when Florence and the doctor's name were first mentioned. Berlinger went on to talk about the steroid investigation, the list of names, including Derek's, and the phone call received by Chief Hightower. By now Cindy Jones was weeping. She was holding on to her son's arm and dabbing her eyes with a tissue. Wayne Jones was sitting straight up in his chair, stunned, for once unable to say anything.

It only took Berlinger a few more minutes to finish the story of the investigation, concluding with the discovery of steroids and prescriptions during the search of the star athlete's locker. When he finished, the room was silent except for the sound of the mother's crying.

"Derek, you've heard what Mr. Berlinger has reported." Harland said. "I only have one question for you. Is it true?"

The young star looked first at his parents who stared blankly back at their son, not knowing what to say. For the first time, Derek turned toward Motley. "I'm sorry Coach," he blurted out as his face began to cloud. "I had to do it. I needed to get stronger, bigger. We needed to win. I did it for the team, Coach."

Motley glared at his co-captain, then slammed his giant fist down on the table.

"The team? You did this for the team?! You silly, stupid boy. You've ruined yourself and your team. We may have to forfeit all our games. What will I tell your teammates? What will you tell them?" He rose and for a moment Brett thought the big man was going to reach across the table and grab Derek by the throat. Brett put his arm around the coach's shaking body, gently guiding him back into his chair.

Harland worked to get the meeting back under control. "Wayne and Cindy, I know this is horrible, heart-breaking news for both of you. It is for all of us. Unfortunately it is all true. I am sure your young man will face the consequences of his actions in the manner you have raised him. Do you have any questions, any at all, for me or the other gentlemen here in this room?"

By now the powerful, small-town banker was trying to comfort his wife and son. When he finally spoke, his voice was just a whisper.

"What happens next? What about the scholarships..."

Berlinger answered. "The NCHSAA board will be meeting very soon, Mr. Jones, probably tomorrow. We must address Derek and Albemarle High's situation at the same time as we do several other athletes and their schools. As I said, the doctor's practice touched a number of lives in both North and South Carolina. Our rules forbid the use of all anabolic steroids and other performance enhancing drugs. It is the use of these drugs by players who compete in a high school football game that our organization will address. Derek will not play again for Stanly High. Regarding any college scholarships, I have no say or control over that one way or the other. Assuming your son is able to clean himself up and never use steroids again, I would hope someone will give him a second chance."

Derek spoke to his father, his voice trembling. "I'm sorry, Dad. It's all my fault."

Wayne Jones nodded. He spoke gently to his son. "I know, Derek. You deserve to be punished and face the consequences of what you did. Accept it like a man. Learn from it. And yes, your mother and I will face this together with you." Jones looked back at Harland. "I don't have any more questions right now, Charles. Can I call you later? Right now, I need to take my family home."

"Yes, Wayne, of course. And please keep in mind we have some excellent counselors here that can work with Derek -- work with all of you - - to help get through this terrible situation." Jones nodded but didn't respond.

With that, Harland looked around the room.

"Gentlemen, I believe this meeting is over."

Wayne Jones walked out of the room, one arm around his wife, and the other holding tight to the son he loved and did not want to lose.

7

A CARD AND A LETTER

B rett needed answers. That afternoon, when classes were over, he headed for the school library before football practice, looking for articles dealing with anabolic steroids and sports.

Brett shook his head as he sat down in front of a stack of health and sports magazine articles on performance enhancing drugs. He could only recall one instance he was even "invited" to try steroids. It had happened while rehabbing his shoulder after surgery when a stranger approached Brett at the health club where he was working out. The man said he was a friend of a former Braves teammate. Brett had no idea who the guy was.

"I can help you speed up your recovery. Get you back on the mound sooner," the man said confidently.

Brett asked the stranger what he had. He recognized it as one of the banned substances they had been told about in spring training during their orientation sessions on illegal drugs.

"No thanks. I'm doing fine on my own."

Brett began poring over the magazine articles. He made some notes to take back to his students, particularly the football and baseball teams. *What could be done? What could he do?* Brett gathered his notes and walked down the hallway to his coach's office. This was going to be rough.

As Berlinger predicted, the news of a steroid scandal in high school football spread quickly through the Carolinas. In the little town of Albemarle, the entire community was rocked by the revelations reported in the local newspaper. TV crews from Charlotte and other big Carolina cities descended on Stanly County High School asking questions and looking for answers. They seized on the facts that the school and their star linebacker, Derek Jones, were square in the center of the controversy, along with eleven other Carolina high schools and fifteen of their athletes...a controversy created by horrible misjudgment and the help of a Florence physician.

That they were not the only school affected by the scandal and subsequent investigations did little to ease the pain and hurt felt by the town. This was their team and Derek was their boy, a model student and star on the playing field. Derek was someone you should be like when you get on the playing field at Stanly High. How could this have happened in their community?

The rulings on the steroid scandal by the North Carolina High School Athletic Association were swift and sure. All players were suspended from playing any sports, including football for the remainder of the school year. Senior student athletes like Derek Jones were done playing high school sports. The underclassmen named in the investigation would have an opportunity to apply for reinstatement in the following year. In addition, schools including those not involved in the scandal were ordered to institute information sessions on the dangers of steroids. All students, even the non-athletes, were required to attend.

As far as playing the game of football, Brett was surprised when he learned that Stanly High would be allowed to participate in the state playoffs. "They found that there was no sense punishing the rest of the kids," was Darnell's explanation upon returning with Principal Harland from the emergency meetings in Raleigh.

So Motley, Brett, and the other coaches spent the next days trying to prepare their team for a state playoff football game while dealing with TV and newspaper reporters from throughout the region. They had heard a rumor that ESPN would be showing up on one high school campus. Everyone was relieved when Friday night finally arrived without a sign of the mega sports broadcasting company at Stanly High.

Darnell did his best to lift the players up and get them ready to play, but they could see what Brett was seeing. Their coach was hurting, too. The Wildcats started the game as if in a fog and soon found themselves down 28-0 against Alamance County. They fought back in the second half to get close at 35-21. But at the end it was as if all the energy and emotion had been sapped out of the team and its fans. The season was over.

———•《()》•———

With the end of football, Brett could turn his attention to working out after school in preparation for spring training with the Braves. Most afternoons Darnell joined him. Together they would work out their bodies while trying to reconcile in their minds what had happened to their football season, each determined to be better and stronger in their own way in the coming year.

"You know, Brett, for a long time I was beating myself up. Like I should have seen it coming, should have known something was going on with Derek." The big man put down the barbells and let out a huge sigh. "I don't know. You do the best you can looking after forty young men. But you miss the big one, and it's right in front of you."

"I know what you mean, Darnell. Looking back, I remember thinking Derek appeared to be a lot bigger and stronger than when I saw him last year, but that was it. He didn't act strange or have any signs of steroid use that you read about. Nobody suspected anything."

"I know, but it still hurts."

And so it went for Brett as he worked his way through the strangest and saddest off-season since joining the Braves. Teach at school during the day, then off to his workouts. Everything he did in his exercise program was dedicated to getting his shoulder stronger. Three days a week he would throw outside with Darnell for twenty minutes. The North Carolina winters were usually mild enough that he could pitch off the mound, nice and easy, just to stay loose. On the days he didn't throw, Brett hit the weight machines, making sure he worked his legs as hard as his shoulder and upper body.

"A strong arm with weak legs is useless, Brett," Darnell would admonish his younger friend. Brett reluctantly agreed and with the big man standing over him pushed his body as hard as he ever had in any winter season. The letter from the Braves would be arriving in early January...inviting him to the big club's spring training camp he hoped. He would be ready. This could be his last chance. He would be prepared to give it his best shot, and Darnell was with him the whole way.

The days passed quickly, and Christmas was approaching. The holidays were a happy time at the Davies' home and Brett enjoyed being there with his mother and her family. Elizabeth Davies was the youngest of four children with two older sisters and one older brother. With Brett away most of the year playing baseball, it was the only time for the rest of the family to get caught up on his pro career. Brett's cousins were all married now, and they and their growing families were anxious to hear about his life with the Braves. They were all confident he was on his way to big league stardom.

"I'm not really on the Atlanta Braves yet," Brett would try to explain. "I'm still in the minors." But his protests didn't hold up, his words drowned out by encouragement from Team Davies.

"You will be this year, Brett."

"Do you want me to call them, Uncle Brett? I'll tell them you're their best pitcher."

"They can't win it without you, young man."

All of the extended Davies families were big-time Atlanta Braves fans. Brett was careful every year to get an exact record of all the kids in each of his cousins' families. It only took a quick phone call to the Killian household in early December to provide Chuck with a summary of ages and sizes for each boy and girl, and the major portion of Brett's Christmas shopping was done. Chuck took care of getting the required number of Braves hats, shirts, pictures, auto-graphed baseballs, and anything else they could think of boxed up and sent to the Davies home in plenty of time for Christmas.

Being around her brother and sisters' families made Mrs. Davies even more proud of the little family she and Brett shared. And it was also without fail every Christmas season that she would take her son aside, hand him an envelope, and say with a smile, "This is for you, Brett. It's from your father."

When he was younger, the envelopes usually contained a Christmas card with a small but reasonable amount of money that Brett would take to a favorite store and (with his mother's approval) spend it on something he had been wishing for. In his teenage years there would be a gift certificate for his favorite sporting goods store in Charlotte. Now as he got older, his father might send a gift card for one of the upscale men's clothing stores in the big city. Brett would open the envelope and for a few brief moments think about the hands that had addressed the card and written, "Love, Dad" on the inside. There was someone out there thinking about Brett Davies who he had never met. *His father...who was he? Where was he? Why couldn't they meet?*

Brett had tried when he was younger but eventually realized it was no use continuing to ask his mother those questions. "I'm sorry, Brett. It's just not possible," was all she offered and that was that. So this year as he opened the card from his father and silently read its contents, *"I'm proud of you, Son,"* Brett turned and looked at his mother with a smile. "I'd rather have the sporting goods card."

After the holidays Brett could start to feel the tension build-ing inside him. *Where was the letter?* He didn't want to phone the Braves' office and talk directly to Morey, but he did feel comfort-able talking to Chuck.

"How ya' doing, old man? I got an e-mail from Darnell; he tells me you're finally getting in shape. I bet your mom's cooking put twenty pounds on you by now. It would me."

Brett grimaced. *Good ol' Darnell.* "I haven't gained that twen-ty yet, Chuck, Darnell's working me too hard. I think I'm getting muscles on my muscles. Of course, that's only if he doesn't kill me first."

"How's Darnell doing? That steroid crap had to be hard on him as well as you." Chuck knew Motley well. They had met several years back when Darnell came down to the Braves' Class A team in Macon to check on his old high school buddy. Brett made the introductions between the big man and Chuck, and they quickly became good friends. When he made it to the majors, Chuck always made sure tickets were waiting for Darnell and his family when they visited Atlanta each summer to watch the Braves. With Brett, the three athletes formed an informal, but strong, support team that was always there when one of them needed a friend.

"Well, it was rough on all of us, Chuck, I can't deny that. It caught Darnell and me off guard because Derek was such a great kid."

"Yeah, but there's a lot of scum out there waiting to mess our kids up. I've had people try to give me that stuff. I threw them and their junk out."

Brett decided to change the subject. "Let me ask you something, Chuck. I'm getting a little nervous. It's almost mid-January and I haven't gotten my contract yet. Have you heard anything? You know Morey made it sound like..."

"I know, Brett. Believe me; I've put in a word, actually several words, with the skipper and Morey on your behalf. I can't read what they're thinking. Heck, old man, they ought to give you a shot. We both know that, and they need to do it now. After all, you'll be heading to the rocking chair on the front porch of the old folks' home before too long."

"Thanks for the encouragement."

It didn't take long for Brett to get his answer. The cell phone was ringing as he got into his car following another long work out with Darnell. It was his mother.

"Brett, you have a letter here from the *Atlanta Braves*."

"I'll be right home."

He raced his car down the hill from the high school and five minutes later sped into the driveway of his mother's home. He ran quickly up the front steps and into the living room. An envelope with the Braves logo was lying on the coffee table. Opening it, Brett pulled out two folded pieces of paper. Brett scanned the first document. It was his contract. He was assigned to the AAA Richmond team. *At least that's a step up from Greenville.* He quickly noted the salary offer and then unfolded the second document.

ATLANTA BRAVES BASEBALL
SPRING TRAINING SCHEDULE
LAKE BUENA VISTA, FLORIDA

Pitchers and catchers are to report to spring training headquarters in Lake Buena Vista, Florida no later than 6 p.m. Sunday, February 15.

The rest of the information was a blur to Brett. What to bring, where to stay, who to call with questions. His eyes focused on something handwritten at the bottom of the paper.

Congratulations, Brett. This is the opportunity you've asked for and deserve. Make the most of it. I look forward to seeing you in Florida.

William Morey

Brett raced to the kitchen where Mrs. Davies was waiting. *"Mom, Mom. I'm going to spring training with Atlanta."* He picked her up and they spun happily around the room. "I've got to call Chuck...and Darnell, too. Man, this is it *and I'm ready.*"

Brett Davies was ready. But he didn't know he would soon be starting out on the most memorable season of his baseball career.

8

TRUNKFUL OF MEMORIES

February 14 might be Valentine's Day, but Brett would be leaving for Florida the next day. Brett knew that the drive to the Braves' training headquarters outside Orlando would take about nine hours and he wanted to get down to Chuck's apartment before dark. He made sure his car was packed up and ready to go the night before his early Sunday morning departure. He was careful to put his baseball equipment in a separate bag checking and rechecking to make sure he had everything...glove, spikes, warm-up jersey, stretching band (to loosen his shoulder) Yes, it was all there.

The next morning he was up early. His mother was already in the kitchen making breakfast while also filling a large bag with sandwiches, fruit, chips, bottled water, and other snacks.

"Mom, it's a nine-hour drive not nine days."

"I know Brett, but you can use the rest of the food to stock up your apartment until you have time to go to the store. Is it just you and Chuck living there?"

"Well, for the first few weeks it will be me, Chuck, and Danny Allen our second baseman. Danny is moving to another condo when his family comes down during spring break. Sarah and the kids are coming then, too, but Chuck says I can still stay with them. I guess there will be plenty of room for me and the kids to play and not get in their way."

Brett did not mention that he hoped to still be with the major league camp at that time. Minor league teams started reporting in mid-March. That was the time the first cuts would be made to move players to one of the Braves' minor league teams. Finishing his breakfast, he picked the large grocery bag full of food off the table and headed for the door. It was time to leave.

"Now, Brett, you be careful driving. And don't do anything silly either. Don't make me send Darnell after you."

"Don't worry Mom. Darnell's taken care of me enough. I think I can manage on my own." He lifted her up and spun his mother around the room one more time. "I love you, Mom. Thanks for everything."

Mrs. Davies smiled at her boy and gave him a quick kiss on the cheek. "I love you too, Brett. And I'm so proud of you. We all are. Now you call as soon as you can and let me know what's happening. Everyone will be asking."

"Don't worry, Mom. I'll call you tonight after I check in at camp and get over to Chuck's place."

Brett settled into his car, easing it out of the driveway and toward the roads that led to Orlando. There was not much Sunday morning traffic. Before long he was past Charlotte heading south on I-77 to Columbia. Brett wanted to use the long drive as a time to think over everything that had happened in the off-season, clear his mind, and prepare for what lay ahead at the Braves spring training camp.

The past months had been busy with school, working out, and of course the annual "spring cleaning in February" at the Davies' home. His mother's words still rang in his ear. "We have to do it now, Brett. You're not going to be here to help me in March or April." Brett enjoyed this yearly ritual with his mother, but he was careful not to let her know. They always came across old family photos or some of Brett's sports awards and other trophies from his Albemarle school days. It was fun for both of them to stop their cleaning and packing for a few moments and reflect happily on those earlier times together.

One day, Brett was moving a large trunk his mother wanted

transferred from the garage to the attic. It was packed full, and Brett knew there was no way he could get it up the stairs by himself. "Hey, Mom, come give me a hand with this." Brett set the trunk down and opened the lid to view its contents. The trunk was filled with large heavy books as well as bags of clothing. Brett had never seen any of it before.

Elizabeth Davies was excited. "Oh, my goodness. That's my cheerleading outfit from high school. And that's my math book, oh how I hated Algebra. Look, here's my eleventh grade English book. Mrs. Ditmar was my teacher."

Brett gazed at his mother as she dove deep into the trunk's memories. Her eyes sparkled with delight as she examined books, pictures, and clothing that had been hidden almost thirty years. "Here are my class yearbooks, Brett. Let's see, this must be my junior year."

She handed the dusty book over to Brett while reaching for another. Brett opened to the index looking for where his mother's picture would be found. She was on several pages, cheerleading, school newspaper, as well as the individual photos of the junior class. "Isn't this a picture of you and Aunt Susie?"

Mrs. Davies looked over her son's shoulder and laughed at the black and white photo of two young girls with long blond hair. "Leave that out, Brett. I'll make sure Susie gets over here soon to see this."

Brett put the yearbook down and noticed an envelope sticking out from the pages. He pulled it out for closer inspection and found it held a plastic bag with a yellow rose, wilted but petals still attached. "What's this, Mom?"

"Oh that's the corsage I wore to our prom. I remember Susie and I double dated that night. I think that was the first time your grandparents let me stay out after midnight. But, of course, they were still awake waiting for me when I got home."

Brett chuckled. He remembered Grandma and Grandpa Davies and was quite sure they had the lights on for their youngest daughter. He turned the envelope over and noted some faded writing scribbled in one corner. *"To Lizzie, all my love."* Next to it was a Valentine drawn with the initials *JF+ ED* inside the heart.

"Wow, Mom, you had a boyfriend!"

Mrs. Davies blushed. "He took me to the prom, Brett. Everyone needed a date. It wasn't a big deal."

"Yeah right... All my love, Lizzie." Brett picked his mother up and swung her around. "And I thought I was your only guy," he teased.

"You are, Brett, you are. Now put me down before the Braves' next star pitcher injures his back."

Brett stopped at a roadside park near the South Carolina-Georgia border to eat his lunch. It was a warm day for February, and he was heading south. Those trunks held lots of memories for his mother. *What's gonna be inside my trunk? When will I find someone to share memories with?* He closed his eyes, enjoying the feel of warm sunshine and hint of spring not far away. *Enough of that. This is my chance to make the major leagues. Concentrate on your job and show Morey you deserve to stay.*

He returned to his car and continued south into Georgia, next stop Orlando, Florida. The miles flew by as Brett pondered his past and his future. Crossing into Florida, he checked his watch. He was making good time. He would be checking in at Braves' headquarters in about three hours and be able to get over to Chuck's condo before dark. Tomorrow would be the first day of spring training with the Atlanta Braves, and Brett Davies had been invited to join them.

9

SPRING TRAINING

Chuck and Danny were already at the condo when Brett arrived. It was good to see his friends (and hopefully teammates) again. The evening was filled with lots of laughter, and talk about families, baseball, and the coming season. Several of the other Braves players had leased units in the same complex and stopped in later that night. Chuck made sure to introduce Brett to the fellows he did not know, and Brett soon found his nervousness about spring training starting to go away. He realized he was not the only one worried about the future.

The evening was drawing to a close when Chuck stood up and asked for his teammates' attention. "Guys, no one is happy with the way last season ended." Brett noticed that all eyes were on the young Braves superstar. "Getting beat out in the seventh game by the Mets...just missing a chance to go to the World Series. Not good, not good at all. But tomorrow a new season starts for all of us. Let's show Morey and Schulz what we're made of. Let's dedicate ourselves to winning our division and winning the playoffs. We do that," Chuck paused and took one last look around the room, "and I really like our chances to win it all. What do you say?"

The players' cheers gave the answer. Last year was over. Tomorrow is a fresh start for the Atlanta Braves. Brett smiled as he watched the reaction to his friend's talk. *Who would've thought? Chuck Killian, leader of men.*

Opening day for spring training dawned sunny and warm, a beautiful February Florida morning. *Definitely a fresh start.* Brett tried to relax as he loaded his gear into Chuck's SUV. He climbed into the back seat, letting Danny ride shotgun, as Chuck headed onto the highway for the short drive to the Braves' complex near Disney World.

Petey was the first to greet Brett as he walked into the clubhouse looking for his locker. "Good to see you here, Brett. You eat those batters up, young man. I wanna see you in Atlanta. We gotta beat those darn Yankees." Petey was off and running on another tirade about free agent spending and the advantage big city teams like New York have over everyone else. Brett just smiled and reached out his hand. "Thanks, Petey. I need all the support I can get."

Brett found his cubicle and started unpacking his equipment bag. He examined the Atlanta uniform hanging on one of the hooks. Holding the jersey up, he turned it around and ran his fingers over the letters on the back D A V I E S. He saw that he had been given number 72. *I might be on the roster, but they got me pretty far down. Guess that's about right for now.*

The daily schedule had been placed in each player's locker. The first day started with a team meeting on Field #1 at 9:00 a.m. Brett glanced at his watch and saw that he had enough time to get his uniform on, look around a little bit, and get out on the field. The rest of the day was a combination of physical exams, stretching, jogging, batting practice, and player meetings by position. They had a one hour lunch break and would be finished by 4:00 p.m.

"Hey, Brett, we might have a chance to get nine holes in." Brett looked up and saw Chuck was standing next to him looking over the schedule. Brett had brought his golf clubs to Florida but wasn't sure he could afford to play every day, even if the schedule did give him time. "Maybe so, Chuck, maybe so."

"OK, let's plan on it. I've got some passes for cart and greens fees out at Little River. The guy I'm renting the condo from gave them to me."

"Sounds good, Chuck. The price is right for sure." Brett smiled and headed out onto the field for the meeting. *Big league perks.*

The GM and Braves skipper were already on the field engrossed in conversation along the first base line. Petey instructed all the players to sit up in the grandstand behind the dugout. Morey spoke first. He talked about the Braves' history, the owner's financial support, and the belief of the Atlanta community that this would be their year. "Men, at this point, what I and the rest of our front office may do -- or not do -- is somewhat irrelevant. We've got great facilities and gathered tremendous fan support. Most importantly, we've invested in you. Our payroll this year is ranked in the top five of all major league clubs. But when you step onto the field, that doesn't matter, either. What matters is your performance and winning results. We've set the table...it's up to each of you to get it done. That's what we expect. Good luck, gentlemen."

There was a brief silence and then some polite applause from the players. Brett joined in. *Good ol' Morey. He has a way of getting right to the point.* Schulz was a man of fewer words. His brief talk followed closely on what Chuck had said at the condo the night before, including the heartbreaking loss to the Mets in the final game of the playoffs.

"But this is a new year, boys. Let's use these next six weeks to get our minds and bodies ready for a tough and successful season. Now most of you look like you're already in pretty good shape." He paused and surveyed the group. "Except for you, Jamison. Good lord, son, did you have a fork and spoon in your hands all winter?"

With that, the players broke up into hysterical laughter, a few yelling out, "Cleo, Cleo, Cleo!" Everyone knew that their slugging left fielder, Cleo Jamison, liked to eat. Spring training would be a challenge as the big man struggled to "slim down" to under 250 pounds on his 6' 3" frame. Schulz tried to regain control.

"All right, everyone quiet down. Seriously, let's get in baseball shape while we're down here. We've got six weeks. I don't need a bunch of sore arms and pulled hammies. OK, Petey, tell them where to go next."

The schedule called for position meetings with each group -- pitchers, catchers, infielders, and outfielders. Physical exams would start at the same time taking each player in alphabetical order. Brett pulled the schedule out of his back pocket as he stood up and surveyed the players filing out of the seats and heading for the various ball fields at the complex. Close to fifty guys fighting for twenty-five roster spots. It was going to be a battle. Brett was in the D-F group for his physical between 10:00 and 11:00 and saw that he was scheduled to pitch batting practice for fifteen minutes starting at 2:30 later that afternoon. Other than that, meetings, calisthenics, jogging. and shagging fly balls would fill Brett's first day of spring training with the Atlanta Braves.

The time passed quickly. Brett's arm and shoulder felt a little tight as he started loosening up for batting practice. He had not thrown a baseball since earlier that week back in Albemarle. He decided to be careful, as Schulz had instructed everyone to be smart. He took the mound and started throwing easily to his first batter, one of several minor league prospects gathered around the cage. He concentrated on a smooth motion and throwing good hittable pitches. Brett noticed Morey and Schulz stopped by the field and watched for a few minutes as he threw. At the end of fifteen minutes, Braves pitching coach Mack Simpson came out to the mound, followed by Jimmy Byrd, one of the team's top pitching prospects. Brett knew Byrd was 16-5 at Richmond last year with an ERA under four. Everyone felt he was ready to go north with the big club when the season started.

"Good job for the first day, Davies." Simpson patted Brett on the back and motioned for Byrd to take over as the two of them walked off the field together. "How's the shoulder feel?"

They always ask that. "Fine, Coach. It felt good to work up a sweat."

"Well you'll be doing plenty of that while you're down here. Listen, go out to the outfield and give me ten easy jogs from foul line to foul line. That'll finish your day out here. Then head into the locker room and ask Petey to have one of his guys rub your arm and shoulder down really good. Make sure you get some ice on it before you shower. Ice it for at least twenty minutes. One day at a time, my boy. We'll see you tomorrow morning 9:00 a.m. sharp." Brett grabbed his warm-up jacket and headed to the left field foul pole. *No one rubbed my arm down in the minors, had to ice it myself. I could get use to this big league treatment.*

Brett decided to pass on golf with Chuck later that afternoon. He wanted to be extra cautious about handling aches and pains after the first workout. It was not till later that evening that he had a chance to catch up with Chuck and Danny on their first day. Back at the condo, Chuck fixed dinner for his two roommates (he was a surprisingly good cook), and afterward they sat down in the large family room to watch some TV. It had been a long first day. "Always is when you're not playing, just practicing," Chuck observed.

"Well we should start having some intra squad games soon," Danny commented. "Then our first exhibition game is March 1, that's less than two weeks away. And guess who? The Mets."

The three looked at each other, and then Chuck replied. "I guess that means it'll be déjà vu all over again, doesn't it?"

Brett spoke up next. "I counted twenty pitchers out there when we had our first meeting with Mack. I figure they plan on taking ten, maybe eleven to Atlanta and I know for sure who seven of them will be, so that means...."

"For crying out loud, Brett. You're thinking way too much. Just go out there and pitch."

"Well thank you, Mr. Killian. You certainly have an interesting way of keeping everything in perspective."

The schedule was pretty much the same for the first week. Brett pitched fifteen minutes of BP each day. To his relief, his shoulder continued to feel strong. After a couple days, he started throwing an extra ten to fifteen minutes on the sideline where he could pitch harder than batting practice speed, as well as begin mixing in some curves and change ups. *So far, so good.*

The intra-squad games started the second week. Everyone was assigned to one of four teams, so two nine inning games could be played each afternoon. The rosters were a mixture of veteran players and anxious minor leaguers with no hint of who stood where in the minds of the coaches and executives. Brett, along with the other rookies, knew that this was the first opportunity to show they belonged in Atlanta. *Do well in the scrimmage games, get a shot at pitching in some exhibition games against other major leaguers; do well in that and...just keep going and hope for the best.* The first cuts would come on March 15 when the rest of the minor league players reported. That was less than three weeks away.

Brett's first scrimmage game was uneventful. He pitched one inning, giving up one hit but no runs. The batters were a combination of Atlanta players plus four from last year's Richmond team. Given the experience level of the opposition, Brett rated his performance a solid B. His second outing was not as successful. It was a cool overcast day with a light rain falling. For the first time in two weeks, Brett felt uncomfortable. His arm was tired, his shoulder ached, and he knew he was in for a long afternoon...even if he was only going to be out there one or two innings. He tried to stay positive. *Come on, Davies, you can gut this one out.*

Danny was the first batter he faced. Brett walked his roommate in just five pitches. *Pitching too careful...gotta go after 'em.* Next up was Brett's Greenville teammate, Felix Cardenas. Felix had been impressive last fall during his brief outing with the Atlanta team after the AA season was over. The word among all the players had Felix as the Braves' starting shortstop, maybe even this season. Brett was concentrating hard. He did not want any more walks, but his first pitch -- a fastball -- wasn't fast enough. Cardenas ripped a double into the gap between left and center scoring Danny. It quickly got worse. An error, another walk, and a single plated the second run of the inning before Brett could finally get two outs on a long fly to left and a fielder's choice. Chuck was up next, runners on first and third.

Brett's shoulder was killing him. He cursed the gloomy gray skies and prayed for warm Florida sunshine. Nothing. *OK, I'll have to be real smart here.* Pitching carefully, he worked his way into a hole with a 3-1 count. Brett was determined to not give in as Chuck stared impassively at his friend on the mound. He could tell Brett was hurting, but he also knew his buddy was a battler. Brett wound up and fired a sidearm fastball aiming for the inside corner of the plate. He missed. Chuck didn't. Some day they would be able to laugh and talk about that pitch...but not today. The ball took off on an arc from Chuck's bat rising over the 365 foot sign in left center. To Brett, it appeared to still be on the way up as it sailed over the palm trees behind the fence. Three more runs scored.

Thankfully the next batter swung on Brett's first pitch and popped out to the Braves first baseman, Angel Matias. Brett trudged slowly off the mound. Looking up he saw Morey getting up from his seat behind the dugout and head to the other field. Brett's intra-squad team manager, Jamey Skiles, who was slated for the same position this season with the Class A team in Rome, Georgia, patted Brett on the back.

"Tough day, Brett. That'll happen sometimes. Go get your running in and let 'em work on your arm back in the training room. Tomorrow's another day." Brett nodded, grabbed his jacket and headed to the outfield.

The next morning Petey and some of the other trainers continued working on Brett's shoulder. It was a warm day which, along with the rub down and ice, was making his arm feel a lot better. Brett checked the schedule and saw that he was on Chuck's team today, but not listed to pitch.

"What do you think that means, Chuck?"

"I don't know, old man. Maybe they're afraid of losing too many balls over the palm trees. That could get expensive, you know"

"Very funny."

"Laugh or cry, Brett. Laugh or cry. Besides your arm could probably use the rest, right?"

Brett nodded and started removing the wrapping that held the ice pack to his shoulder. "You're right, Chuck. It wouldn't hurt to lay off a day."

Brett decided if he wasn't going to pitch, he would push hard that morning, working his legs with lots of sprints, squats, and other exercises. The pitchers were also scheduled for some fielding practice, picking up bunted balls, covering first, and other game situations they all knew could mean the difference between a win or a loss in a future contest. The day was warm and sunny, and he enjoyed being able to sweat out the frustration from the previous afternoon.

After the morning workout, he went back to the clubhouse to put on a dry shirt and then headed over to the dining hall for lunch. He had a "good tired" feeling and looked forward to watching Chuck and his teammates in the afternoon. He would spend part of the game in the dugout observing; and then in the later innings do some jogging in the outfield, all the time enjoying the warm sunshine of the Florida winter day.

Brett got to the field and saw that Skiles had been assigned as their team manager. Jamey was only a few years older than Brett, but he was already starting his fifth year of coaching in the Braves organization.

"How come you ended up coaching before you were thirty?" Brett asked.

"Injuries, Brett. I couldn't get over them. I tore my knee up sliding into second, had surgery but...I was a catcher. I tried, but I just couldn't get it done. All the squatting down and trying to block pitches. Just trying to run got ridiculous, limping down to first. No, I lasted another couple years. Then for reasons I still don't know, they thought I could be a good coach. So, four years ago, Morey asked me to come down here and work with some of the young guys in the Winter Development League. I did OK, I guess. Then they had me manage our Rookie League team up in Danville. I did that for two years. We had some good talent and won the championship each year. A lot of those kids are in camp now. Cardenas and Byrd were both on my Danville teams. Bet you didn't know that?"

"I had no idea."

"Anyway, last year I managed in Rome, and I'll be going back this season." He paused and looked closely at Brett. "At least I'm still in the game. Maybe this is the way I can help the Braves win the World Series. Who knows?"

Brett listened intently to the young manager's story. *Jamey is only a few years older than me. Morey told me he thought I had a gift for coaching and teaching.... that the Braves needed coaches and managers with that gift.*

"So how do you feel today, Brett? You didn't look comfortable out there yesterday."

"Ah, it was just one of those days, Jamey. Sometimes it takes a while to get my shoulder loose. Warmer days help a lot, that's for sure."

"Yeah, I heard about you hurting your shoulder. Tough break, I've been there. I remember watching you throw one time about three years ago. You were really bringing the heat then."

Brett knew what Jamey was talking about. "Yeah, now I just have to pick my spots to throw that 95 mph stuff." The young manager laughed at the old minor leaguer's joke and slapped Brett on the back.

"Hang in there, Brett. You'll be fine no matter what happens."

Brett headed to the outfield to do some easy long tosses before the game started. The scrimmages would be over soon. The exhibition season would begin in just three days against the hated Mets. Even the veterans were starting to get a little more serious.

The game turned into the Chuck Killian show as the Braves' young slugger went three for three, hammering two long home runs beyond the palm trees. Brett was jogging in the outfield when Chuck's second shot left the park over his head.

"Haven't I seen that before, Jimmy?"

Byrd had given up Chuck's first home run. He paused long enough to follow the flight of the ball as it sailed over the fence. "Yes, Brett, I believe several of us have seen exactly that."

"Well good, maybe if he hits enough of them, they'll forget who pitched"

On Friday morning the Braves posted the rosters for their two exhibition teams. Each listed twenty-five players for the games that would start the following day. Most of the "Atlanta" roster looked suspiciously like last year's major league team with a few highly touted recruits thrown into the mix to see how they would do. The second team, listed as the "Braves", was mostly younger prospects probably going to Richmond or Greenville in a couple weeks, some reserves from last year's big league team, and a few players coming off injuries. Brett was on the Braves.

"Congratulations, old man. You've survived the first two weeks. Now you have an opportunity to shine."

"Better make it a bright light, Chuck. I'm pretty far down on that list."

"Just do your thing, Brett. These exhibition game rosters change a lot before final cuts are made, especially with pitchers. Just make sure you're ready."

Fair enough. I asked for it, and now I've got it. This is my chance to prove myself to Morey and the rest of them.

10

BIG LEAGUE OPPORTUNITY

There were several major league teams training within a two hour drive of the Braves' complex in Lake Buena Vista. For many of the veteran players the short bus rides in March brought back distant memories of never-ending road trips from their time in the minors. Six hours or more from city to city was far too common. It was just one of many motivating factors for staying on the big team with jet travel, clubhouse attendants, and liberal meal money. But now, in spring training, everyone traveled by bus, including Brett and the rest of the Braves' B team players. They were heading for the Houston Astros' spring training headquarters in Kissimmee. Chuck's A (for Atlanta) team was playing the Mets back at the Braves' Park, so today was Brett's turn to travel.

Greenville manager, Jimmy Graham, oversaw the B team with Skiles as his assistant. Brett was glad to see that his friend and bullpen coach, Frankie Simmonetti, was also on the staff.

"Just like old times in Greenville, isn't it, Brett?" Frankie was excited they were at last playing someone else, no more intra-squad games. "Except the weather is a tad better this time of year."

It was indeed a beautiful Florida day for baseball. Warm sun and clear skies, and the gusty winds that normally prevailed in March were non-existent.

"I think you're right, Frankie." Brett was standing in the bullpen looking out on the field of play. The first game was moving along, already in the fifth inning. "However, I believe we have a little more company out here than we had in Greenville."

Each of the Braves' exhibition teams had ten pitchers on their roster. All but the starter, top prospect Byrd, were in the bullpen when the game began. It was most definitely crowded.

Jimmie pitched a strong three innings, holding the Astros to just one run while striking out four. Jerry Feiler, who was entering his third season as an Atlanta starter, pitched the fourth and fifth innings, giving up a home run to Damion Ortiz, the Astros' star first baseman, but nothing else. The concept was to use five of the ten pitchers each day depending on the game situation. Starters were expected to extend their pitch count and go further as the exhibition season wore on, while those slated for middle and short relief, like Brett, would pitch an inning or two every other day. Graham told Brett that he would be going in for the eighth inning today.

The score was tied 2-2 after Feiler retired the Astros in the fifth. But in the next two innings, the bats for both teams came alive. It was 8-7 Houston when Brett headed to the mound to pitch the bottom of the eighth. He was glad to see that Braves back-up catcher, Billy Kowalski, was behind the plate. After Brett finished his warm-up tosses, Billy walked out to the mound to review signals.

"You're looking good, Brett. Just relax and watch my locations. I know these guys pretty well, so just trust me."

"Sounds good, Billy. I don't have a scouting report on any of them. You're the boss, that's for sure."

"No problem. Remember pitching against Chuck during batting practice last year? Just like that, my man, just like that!"

Brett picked up the resin bag to dry his sweaty palm. The day seemed much hotter as he stood alone in the middle of the diamond. Turning to face the batter, he toed the rubber, took a deep breath, and looked in for the sign. *This is it. Time to show them I belong.* He hadn't seen Morey in the stands but knew other Braves scouts and front office staff were there ready to report back. *Can't worry about that crap. Gotta concentrate. One pitch at a time.*

Billy signaled for a fastball and moved his glove to the outside corner of the plate. The Astros batter, Willie Thompson, was also a rookie. Brett figured they were both nervous. He fired the first pitch to the right handed batter, and Thompson fouled it down the first base line. Three pitches later the count stood at two balls and two strikes. Brett was feeling calmer with every pitch, focusing on the task in front of him. He looked in for Billy's signal and was pleased to see they were thinking alike. He had thrown four straight fast balls; time for an off-speed curve. Billy moved to the outside of the plate, keeping his target low

Brett concentrated on presenting the same pitching motion and arm speed until the time of release, flicking his wrist for the curve as he hurled the ball to the center of the plate. The ball was traveling just a little slower than Brett's previous pitches, but it was enough to throw Thompson off. As the ball curved over the outside edge of home plate, he lunged at it to avoid a strike-out, tapping an easy grounder to second base. One out.

Brett's arm felt good. *This could be fun.* He faced the second batter of the inning, Manuel Ortista, the Astros' veteran outfielder. *Gotta trust Billy with this guy.* Kowalski called for pitches low in the strike zone, mixing up the location, inside and out. Brett pitched with care but ended up walking Ortista when he bounced a 3-1 curveball in front of home plate. The slugger Ortiz was up next.

Billy got a new ball from the umpire, called time, and walked out to the mound. "We gotta keep it down on him, Brett. Jerry said he hung a curve for the home run. The guy can't run that good anymore, so let's get a ground ball and get out of this."

"Sounds good, Billy. But why is Damion still in the game? It's the eighth inning. Don't they rest their regulars in these games?"

"Don't know, Brett." Billy spit into the dirt, handed the ball to his pitcher, and turned to head back to home plate. "Maybe he knew you'd be pitching."

Everyone's a comedian. Brett decided his strategy would be to go away with his sidearm curve and try to set Ortiz up for something inside. Billy called for a fastball on the outside corner and Brett agreed, but the pitch sailed wide. Ball one. Two side-arm curves later and the count was one ball and two strikes. He had been lucky. The second curve resulted in a towering fly ball down the left field line that turned foul at the last second before sailing into the parking lot.

Didn't fool anyone on that one. Still he had thrown a combination of three pitches all on the outside part of the plate. Ortiz had dived into each one of them. *OK, Billy, let's see if this works.* The catcher called for a fastball, this time moving his target to the inside corner of the plate. Brett took his windup and stepped to the third base side of the mound, dropping his shoulder down in the same motion as the two previous curveball pitches. This time Brett released the ball off his fingertips, getting as much backspin as possible. The pitch headed toward the center of the plate. *Too high, too high.* But then at the last instant it dove in toward the batter. Ortiz swung mightily but the ball was in on his hands resulting in a weak ground ball to the mound. Relieved, Brett gobbled it up and fired to Cardenas at second, who relayed it to first to complete the double play. Jamey was the first to greet him as he got to the dugout.

"Great job, Brett. You handcuffed Ortiz perfectly."

"Yeah, but I got lucky on that one curve. He almost took that one all the way."

"Hey, it went foul, didn't it? That's all that matters. Makes up for the ones that stay fair by six inches."

Brett smiled and slapped his catcher on the back as Billy trotted past. "Good call, Billy. I needed that."

"No problem, Brett. You had to make the pitches. Keep that up and we'll be looking for an apartment together in Atlanta."

Brett sat down in the dugout and pulled on his jacket. Wiping his sweaty face with a towel, his mind flashed back to everything he had done to get to this point. The surgery, rehab, Greenville, working out with Darnell. He just needed to keep going, take it one day at a time. He wondered if Morey and the rest of them noticed. *It doesn't matter. Tonight, I'm calling Mom.*

The days and games passed quickly as spring training for the

Braves' players moved closer to the March 15 "cut down" day. Other roster moves were possible before Atlanta would break camp the first week of April and head north for opening day. Still, everyone knew after four weeks of close observation by the Braves' staff, where you were placed on the fifteenth was pretty much where you were going to start the season.

Brett saw action in several more games leading up to the big day. He pitched well, giving up a few hits and runs. For the most part he was looking good. However, neither he nor Chuck had heard any opinions about Brett from the coaches on the "A" team. The two friends did not know if that was good or bad.

"Just keep going out there when they tell you to, Brett." Chuck always had a way of simplifying things. "If they don't want you to pitch, then *that* would be the time to start worrying."

Graham told Brett that he would be pitching again on Tuesday against the Cincinnati Reds. *"March 13. Anniversary Day,"* Brett thought grimly. It was two years ago on that date when he injured his shoulder. Yet he was glad to get the news. He needed one more good outing before roster moves were made. He also needed to get the bad memories of two years ago behind him. He vowed to accomplish both on Tuesday.

Game day dawned cool and blustery. A light rain was falling as Brett rode into the stadium with Chuck and Danny. The "A" team had the day off, so most of the guys were going to take batting practice and then head for the golf course, hoping the sun would be out by then. Chuck would not be playing golf, as he was still nursing a sprained ankle from catching his spikes while sliding during yesterday's game.

"Keep in mind gentlemen, that even though I sacrificed my body -- well, my ankle anyway--I was in fact safe. And putting Javier in to run for me was very smart, as he ended up scoring the winning run on Cleo's single."

"Yeah, great job, Chuck," Brett shot back. "Tear yourself up for an exhibition game win. Way to go."

"Gotta play 'em all the same, old man. No other way to do it."

He paused for a moment, turning serious. "Make sure you loosen up good out there, Brett. This is an ugly day to play baseball." The rain was falling harder as they neared the stadium.

Brett did some extra running in the outfield, followed by some easy long tosses with Feiler before the game started. The rain had stopped, but the wind still made conditions nasty on the cloudy day.

"Not bad enough to cancel, I guess. Just enough to make it miserable," Frankie moaned as Brett entered the bullpen. Brett pulled his jacket on and fingered the stretching band in the pocket that would help him stay loose until it was time to warm up. He was scheduled to pitch the fifth and sixth innings, so he settled into the ritual of watching the game while at the same time struggling to stay relaxed and ready.

At the start of the fourth inning, Brett motioned to Frankie that it was time. He removed his jacket, stretched one more time, and walked over to the bullpen mound and started tossing to Billy. He was glad that his friend would be going in at the same time to catch Brett's two innings and the rest of the game.

The wind continued to blow hard with no sun in sight. *Feels like it's in the fifties. This isn't good.* Brett's shoulder still felt tight, and his arm was aching. *Not a good combination. Just gotta gut it out today. Throw strikes, get some easy outs, and get to the whirlpool.* He continued to throw, mixing in a few curves. The extra snap on those pitches jolted his shoulder, so he eased up. When the Braves came to bat in their half of the fifth, he took a seat next to Frankie. Brett pulled his jacket on tighter to retain as much body heat as possible.

"How do you feel, Brett?" Frankie asked with a worried frown.

"Oh great, Frankie, fantastic. Just a beautiful day to pitch." They both laughed. They both knew the truth.

The inning ended, and Brett trotted in from the bullpen. Billy trailed behind him.

"Same formula as before, Brett?"

"Shoulder's a little tight, Billy, but we'll get through it."

Brett handed his jacket to the bat boy and toed the rubber. He finished his warm-up pitches and surveyed the sparse crowd as Billy tossed the ball down to second. Chuck had finished his ankle treatment and was sitting in the stands behind the Braves' dugout along with a few other teammates. Schulz and Morey were sitting directly behind home plate surveying all the action, taking notes, and talking quietly. *This is it. Last chance to show them I belong.*

Billy walked out to the mound to go over the signals with his pitcher. "Good luck, Brett. I know most of these guys. Just follow my lead again, OK?" Brett nodded and took the ball from Billy's hand. It was time.

The first batter was the Reds' second baseman, Torey Helms. Billy signaled for a fastball, which Helms promptly ripped down the left field line but luckily a few inches foul. *I've got nothing today. What am I gonna do?* Three mediocre fastballs later the count stood at 2 balls and 2 strikes. Even though a cold wind was blowing, Brett was sweating. His aching shoulder was finally feeling a little better.

OK Billy. Time for something different, Brett muttered to himself. *Let's go with the curve.* As if reading his mind, Billy flashed two fingers for the signal. Brett nodded, took a deep breath, and began his wind up. Striding toward home plate, he released the ball overhand with a hard snap of the wrist, desperate to put as much spin on the ball as possible.

The pain was immediate. Brett felt a knife-like jab cutting into his shoulder. He fell to the ground, clutching his right side in agony. Billy rushed out to him.

Brett! Are you Ok?

Brett got up onto one knee, still grasping his throbbing shoulder. The pain began to subside, but he could feel the tears of frustration welling up in his eyes.

"I don't know. It felt like somebody stabbed me in the shoulder." He looked around, embarrassed that he had fallen and a sinking realization of what had just happened.

Jamey was the second to reach him. Chuck and his bad ankle had climbed out of the stands and was rushing towar his friend.

"Come on, old man." Chuck grabbed Brett around the waist and helped him to his feet. "Let's get you into the training room and figure out what happened." Brett looked into the stands and saw Morey and Schulz staring out at him, taking the scene in.

"Chuck, this can't be happening now. Not after all..."

"Easy, Brett. Let the doc tell us what's happened, OK?" Chuck was walking his friend off the field. Somebody got Brett's warm-up jacket off the bench and draped it over his shoulder. "We'll get some X-rays taken. Then we'll deal with whatever we have facing us."

Petey drove up behind the dugout in a golf cart, and the two players climbed on for the ride back to the training facility. No one said a word. The Braves' trainer, Mickey O'Brien, met Brett at the door. He had already received a call from Jamey as to what happened. "Sit up on this table, Brett. Let's see what we've got."

Brett gingerly removed his jacket. The pain in his right shoulder had lessened to a dull ache, but his whole right side trembled from the shock. O'Brien took Brett's right hand and began extending the pitcher's arm up, out, and down, probing various points, starting from the elbow, and working his way up to the shoulder.

"How's this feel? How about here? Lift your arm straight up." Brett grimaced when the trainer pushed around the scar from his surgery. "In there, huh? Try rotating your arm around, sort of like a windmill."

Brett raised his arm, but as he reached back, the pain returned. "Can't do it, Doc. That's where it hurts. Same spot as before."

"OK, Brett. Tell you what. Let's take some X-rays of your shoulder. If we see something interesting, we'll send you downtown for an MRI. We may want to do that anyway just to get a complete picture."

Brett nodded and looked up at Chuck, who was standing next to the door. "Same day, Chuck. Same place. Just a different year." His friend remained silent. They could only wait to see what the X-rays showed, hoping for good news.

The Braves training facility was well equipped with a wide range of diagnostic equipment. It only took a few minutes for the pictures of Brett's shoulder to be developed.

"Brett, I believe there aren't any tears. Tendons and ligaments appear to all be intact. You can see a lot of scar tissue that remains around where your shoulder was repaired a couple years ago. My guess is you just felt some of that breaking loose. At least that's what I think happened. Let's get your shoulder wrapped up in ice, and we'll see what the MRI tells us. Chuck, I assume you'll be driving. Right?"

The big slugger nodded.

"OK. The MRI will be at the Orlando Ortho Center this afternoon. Here's a map on how to get there. I'll call them so the staff knows you're coming."

The next day dawned clear and warm, a beautiful spring day in Florida. *Why did I have to pitch yesterday?* Brett sighed. He was sitting in the training room waiting for Mickey. O'Brien had told him they should have his MRI results right after lunch. It was now fifteen minutes past one. Brett stood up and paced around the room. Just then the trainer walked in, a large manila envelope under his arm.

"Hi, Brett. Let's find somewhere we can sit down and go over this."

He motioned for Brett to follow him down a short hallway to a meeting room with several chairs arranged around a large rectangular table, along with a TV, DVD player, and viewing screens for examining the radiology pictures. Brett sat down across from Mickey as the trainer took the MRI pictures out of the envelope and began hanging them on one of the illuminated screens.

"Brett, as you know, an MRI takes a complete picture of an area of the body. We get a lot better look at what's going on than from an X-ray."

Brett nodded. *This is going down hill fast.* "OK, Mickey. I understand. What are you trying to tell me?"

"Come around here and I'll show you."

Brett walked around the table and peered at the pictures. There were numerous slides of his shoulder. He squinted at the film but couldn't make out what he was seeing. The trainer smiled as he saw the pitcher's confusion. "Most of these pictures are quite normal, Brett, but look at this view here."

Brett leaned forward and peered at the one Mickey had indicated. O'Brien pointed to a small dark area on the slide. "Brett, this is your tendon that was surgically repaired. Unfortunately, the MRI shows a small tear right here."

Brett heard what Mickey said, trying to process the information. "Small tear? Is that better than the big tear I had? Can I still pitch? Do I have to have surgery? I can't do that again. What about rehab? I can't..."

"Slow down, Davies. Let's sit down and discuss what this means for you." Brett nodded, took his seat, and shut up. He couldn't believe this was happening again.

"Brett, there are several options for you. Yes, surgery is one of them; but it's the last one. Given time and a good rehab program, which I can give you, the tendon should be able to mend on its own in two months, four max."

"*Four months.* That's the middle of July. The season will almost be over. Who would want me then?" Brett slumped in his chair. "Mickey, what do you think? Am I damaged goods?"

"No, Brett. I am positive that the Braves organization doesn't feel that way at all. In fact, they have a third option for you to consider."

"What are you talking about, Mickey? I need..." A loud knock on the door stopped Brett in mid-sentence. He turned in his chair as three men walked in and sat down around the table with Brett and Mickey. Brett was shocked to see that it was William Morey and Barney Schulz. The third person was Jamey, who nodded at Brett with a grim smile on his face. Brett braced for bad news.

Morey spoke first. "Brett, I'll get right to the point. We've been watching you closely all spring, and for the most part you have done an excellent job. But this injury changes everything. You need to take time to get healthy and hopefully avoid more surgery.

But I don't want you going back to Albemarle." The GM paused. "Do you remember what I told you when we met in my office last September?"

Brett nodded but said nothing. *Just keep listening. Where is all this going?*

Morey looked closely at the troubled hurler. "You have a wealth of baseball experience, Brett, particularly on what it takes to be a major league pitcher in the Braves organization. You did a good job, on an informal basis, helping some of our young pitchers in Greenville last year. We want to formalize that talent of yours. We want you to be one of our pitching coaches this season. You can teach those young minds how to use their young arms. Tell them what they need to know, how to train, how to stay sharp mentally, and how to act on and off the field. And you can work on your rehab program at the same time. If your shoulder heals, as we all hope it will, then we'll sit down and discuss what your options are at that point."

Brett looked over at Jamey who was now beaming. "You mean you want me to go down to Rome and help Jamey as his pitching coach?"

"That's correct, Brett." Morey sat back and waited.

Jamey leaned across the table. "Brett, you're exactly what I need down there. It's Class A, most of our pitchers are going to be 19 or 20 years old. For some, it might be their first year in pro ball. You'll be great with them."

Brett struggled to process everything. *Four months. More rehab...again.* Still, the Braves hadn't given up on him. They were giving him a chance. His dream was still alive. *And coach 19-year-olds? Can I do that, too?* Brett let a little smile go across his face. *Sure, I can.*

His mind was now clear. Things happen for a reason. His mother had always told him that. He stood up and nodded at Morey, Schulz, and then Jamey.

"OK, I'll do it."

11

NEW TOWN, NEW TEAM, NEW ROLE

Rome, Georgia proudly proclaims itself as "where the rivers meet the hills." Founded in the early 1800's, Rome was built at the foot of the Blue Ridge Mountains, around and along the three rivers of Etowah, Coosa, and Oostanaula. The seven hills that rose above the town reminded the founders of another city surrounded by hills, thus the new town was given the name of Rome.

Having survived Sherman's '" March to the Sea'" and the decline of the textile industry, Rome had entered the twenty-first century as the county seat with more than 36,000 citizens. The local Chamber of Commerce worked diligently to market the town's shops and historic building, always pointing out that Rome is only sixty-five miles northwest of downtown Atlanta. It was that proximity that led the Braves organization to relocate their Class A minor league team from Macon to Rome at the start of the 2003 season. Minor league baseball proved to be popular for families who spent an exciting but inexpensive night at their beautiful new ballpark. The five thousand-seat State Mutual Stadium opened in time for their first game.

Brett arrived in his new town a few days ahead of Jamey and the rest of the team. He was to meet with the team's owner and general manager, Kenny Kiser, to make final preparations for the team's arrival and the start of the season on Saturday evening, only three days away. He hoped the field was in good shape and Kiser had everything else ready. Ticket sales, concessions, souvenirs, locker room, and training supplies; the list went on and on. Brett had always taken the "" behind the scenes stuff" for granted. "Just show up and play," he told Kiser. "Things are different now."

Brett spent the last two weeks of spring training working with Jamey and the players assigned to the Rome team, particularly the young pitching staff. His group consisted mostly of second-year players, and they all knew their stay in Rome might be short-lived. The annual baseball draft was coming up in June and would bring top-ranked high school and college players into the Braves organization. Some would be assigned to Rome, leaving no room for those with less ability.

Still Brett was confident his staff had a lot of talent. For the most part, they were receptive to his instruction. He chose to talk a little bit about his time with the Braves, mentioning his shoulder injury as a cautionary tale to always respect the skills with which they were blessed. "Never abuse or take those gifts for granted, guys." Brett thought they understood what he had to say.

"You found a place to live yet, Brett?" Kiser asked at the end of their first meeting. "There are a number of nice apartment complexes here in Rome."

Brett shook his head. Normally he would consider apartment living, but he was tired of the cramped quarters and noisy neighbors. His coaching salary should allow him to look for something better.

"Thanks, Kenny, but after seeing practically every apartment complex in town, I think I'll pass on that option."

Kiser laughed. "At least we've got the housing arrangements for the team worked out. They can deal with apartment living. They're young. Let's just hope they know how to behave."

"Good point. And some of them are just a year out of high school. That's a lot of testosterone to let loose on Rome, Georgia. Anyway, I'm going to try to find a small house I can rent for the summer. A little space to hang out will be a nice change for me.

Jamey told me he was able to get the same house where he and Dotty lived last year. It sounded like a nice area."

Kenny reached into his desk and found a map of the little town. He handed that and the morning paper to his coach. "Here, this should give you a good start. There are a few nice houses for rent. Hope you can find one that works for you."

The next day Brett grabbed the street map and other information on Rome that he had accumulated and headed out of the motel parking lot, seeking his new home. He had been able to spend a few hours riding around the small town and had a pretty good idea where he would like to be. Everything was coming together. The Saturday opening night was only two days away. The rest of the team and coaches would be arriving for their first workout later that afternoon. That gave him all morning to find a place to live.

It was a beautiful warm April morning in Georgia. The azaleas and magnolias were in full bloom, showing their brilliant pink and white colors. Walkers and joggers, along with mothers and baby strollers, seemed to be everywhere. The good citizens of Rome knew what a great day they had ahead of them.

Brett promised himself to get GPS in his next car as he juggled the map and list of houses on his lap. He navigated the Explorer through the streets, taking in the sights and smells of the spring day. His first stop would be an appointment for a small furnished home in what he had determined to be his favorite neighborhood. Plus, it was close to the ballpark. He pulled up to a stop light behind a church minivan. Sounds of kids inside the van singing their favorite songs added to the happiness of Rome's spring morning.

Brett checked him map; confident he was not that far from his destination. *What street do I need to turn onto?* Noting that the light had turned green, he looked down at his map one more time and hit the accelerator.

CRASH!!

The collision snapped Brett's body back into the seat. Papers, pencils, and coffee cups went flying. He slammed his foot on the brakes and looked around, trying to figure out what happened. He saw that the front end of his car had smashed into the back doors of the church van, which had been pushed several feet forward into the busy intersection. Worse, he heard children crying, as well as the muffled voice of the driver who was trying to calm her kids. Turning off his car's ignition, he opened his door and stumbled out. Brett could hear the words clearer now.

Miss Jenny, what happened?

Be quiet, Samantha, and sit back down. Ally, are you OK?

Yes, I think so.

Good. Reilly, Connor-- are you boys all right?

Yes, ma'am.

"All right. Now listen up. No one is bleeding, so I need all of you to settle down and let me find out what's going on. *Somebody's gotta know something.*"

Brett looked into the driver's window and saw the back of the young woman who was talking to the children. Her blonde hair was pulled into a ponytail.

"Excuse me, Miss. Is everything all right?"

The young woman, who he figured to be Jenny, turned around and stared at Brett. "I think we're OK. I'll need to get back to the church and have them looked at." She got out of the van to examine the damage. "I hope I can still drive--who are you?"

"Well, I'm the guy who ran into you. My name is Brett Davies. I saw the light had changed but didn't..."

"Didn't what?" Jenny's eyes flashed. "Didn't see that we had our turn signal on? Didn't see the cars coming through the intersec-tion? Didn't see that we had to wait for those cars before we could turn? What exactly 'Didn't' you, Mr. Davies?" She was moving now, standing directly in front of Brett, looking up at him, her blue eyes glaring. Brett tried to back up, but by now a crowd had gathered. He was trapped.

"Well, no, I mean, yes. I was looking at my map. You see I'm new in town and looking for a place to live so..."

"*Maybe you should be looking where you're going first.*" Someone in the crowd started to laugh. Brett grimaced for more of the onslaught. "Maybe you should pay more attention to your driving. You're just lucky no one was hurt." Jenny looked back inside the van. "At least I hope not."

Brett started to relax. It seemed her anger was starting to subside. Brett thought she was probably scared, too. He guessed she was in her mid-twenties and noted that she was very cute. *Particularly when she's not yelling at me.*

"Let me get you my insurance information." Brett scrambled back to his Explorer, noting that his front bumper was slightly dented, but otherwise fixable. It appeared that Jenny's church van wasn't as fortunate. At a minimum, it would need extensive repairs to the rear doors as well as the bumper. Returning to the scene of his crime, he saw that Jenny was now surrounded by the small crowd that had gathered. And everyone seemed to know her.

How are you, Jenny?

Are the kids OK?

Do you want me to call Dr. Jake?

A police car drove up to the scene. "Can you drive your van, Jenny?" the officer asked. He turned to stare at Brett, figuring him to be the stranger in town that had caused this whole mess.

"Yes, sir. I can drive it. All the kids seem fine, too. Just a little shook up."

"Well good." He got out of the police cruiser and turned to Brett. "How about you, fella? I assume that's your Explorer there. Let's get these cars out of the intersection and get traffic moving again. First, I'll need to take a couple pictures for the record. Then I want Jenny and you to drive your vehicles over there." He motioned to a nearby service station.

Geez, even the police know her. Brett felt doomed but did as the officer requested. He followed Jenny's van over to the station and got out of his car to face the music.

"So what happened over there?" The officer looked at Jenny, then Brett. "And what's your name, son?"

"My name is Brett Davies, sir. The accident was all my fault" Brett was talking fast, hoping Jenny didn't get all fired up again. "I saw the light change but looked down at my map as I hit the gas. I thought the van was starting up, too. I didn't realize she was waiting to turn."

"OK, fair enough. Do you have anything to add to that, Jenny?" Brett braced for the next volley.

"No, just make sure his insurance company pays for the damage. Back Creek Methodist doesn't have the extra money for higher insurance costs, that's for sure. And we need this van, Mr. Davies. You have to get it fixed pronto."

"I will. Don't worry, I'll even pay the deductible. I'm really sorry. Here is my insurance information and cell phone number so you know how to find me. I'm pretty sure they will need two estimates for the repairs before having the work done. How do I get in touch with you?"

Jenny smiled at Brett for the first time. "You want my phone number? Is this normally how you go about meeting new girls?" Brett blushed. He thought she was teasing but wasn't sure.

"You said you were looking at a street map, Mr. Davies?" The officer was looking over his notes.

"Yes sir. I just got into town this week, and I was going out this morning looking for a place to rent for the summer."

"Just the summer? What do you do?"

"I'm the pitching coach for the Rome Braves baseball team. Our first game is Saturday night. If you like, I would be glad to get some tickets for you." Brett looked at Jenny. "Would you and the kids like to go too?"

"My, my. You're a baseball player?" Brett thought Jenny was looking at him a little differently.

"I was until this year. I pitched in the minors for the Braves but hurt my shoulder. They've asked me to coach this year. Maybe my arm will heal. I don't know..." He stopped. *That's enough. Way too much information for now.*

"Say, Brett," the police officer had finished taking pictures. If you could leave a couple of tickets at will-call for me, Sgt O'Malley, I think I and my son -- he just turned eleven. He would love to go."

"Sure, no problem."

Jenny spoke up. "Nice try, Brett, but we already have our tickets for the game. The Braves have a special promotion. It's Youth Night. Didn't your team tell you that? We'll probably have twenty kids and counselors there. Thanks anyway."

Brett grimaced. Youth night...he thought Kenny had mentioned something about that. "OK, maybe some other time."

Jenny took out a church bulletin from the van and jotted her phone number down. "Let me know how many estimates you are going to need. We must get this repaired fast."

"Sure, sure. And if there's anything else I can do to help..."

"There probably will be, Brett. There probably will. We've got a Braves baseball star that owes Back Creek Church a favor. I'm sure Dr. Jake and I will think of something. See you later, Mr. Davies."

With that, Jenny jumped back into the driver's seat of the van and started the engine. He watched her drive off, the sound of children's laughter fading in the distance. Brett got into his Explorer, trying to collect his thoughts. He found his cell phone and dialed the number of the realtor he had the appointment with. After explaining what had happened, they agreed to meet at the first house on Brett's list in ten minutes. This time he got directions.

A few hours and a few houses later, Brett was in possession of the keys to a small older two-story furnished home that the realtor promised was less than ten minutes from the ballpark. The short lease term was not a problem as the house was owned by a college professor who was completing his sabbatical and would be returning to Rome Labor Day weekend. The neighborhood was quiet. The house, with two bedrooms and a full bath upstairs, living room, den and kitchen down, gave Brett plenty of room. The yard was well landscaped with the back yard fenced in. It wouldn't take long to mow. He would enjoy relaxing on the patio. Several well-established oak and pine trees provided plenty of shade during the hot Georgia summer.

It didn't take Brett long to go back to the motel to get his clothes and other personal items, before checking out. He stopped at the local Piggly Wiggly grocery store on the way back to his house and picked up a few things he would need before the Braves' first road trip. After getting everything moved in, the little house was already starting to feel comfortable.

Brett checked his watch and saw that it was time to get over to the field. Jamey was going to be there at two, and the rest of the Braves players were scheduled to arrive later that afternoon for their first workout. Brett was pleased that the realtor was correct, as it only took a few minutes to arrive at the ballpark. Jamey's car was already in the lot. Brett parked his Explorer next to it and headed to the home team's locker room. Jamey was waiting for him with a big bear hug.

"Brett, my man. How you doing? Seems like Orlando was a long time ago, doesn't it?"

Brett laughed. "I don't think Rome can be compared to Mickey World, Jamey."

"And that's not a bad thing, Brett. Rome's a great little town. Our family really enjoyed our time here last summer. The people are very friendly. Wait till you start meeting some of them."

"Oh, I already have, Jamey, believe me, I already have. In fact, I ran into an attractive young lady who is bringing a bunch of kids from her church to the game Saturday night."

"How about that. I didn't know you worked that fast, Brett. So how attractive and how young?"

"It's kind of a long story. Let's just say that when she calmed down, she was real nice." Brett gave Jamey a quick summary of his day's adventure while the manager finished checking out the locker room.

"At least nobody was hurt, right, Brett? And you said she was good looking. Sounds to me like a pretty good day so far. Come on, let's go find Kenny and see how the field is shaping up. I've told the team to report here at five. We'll stretch them out after their long car rides and then get some hitting and fielding in. We'll turn the lights on, too; see if there are any dark spots out there. Your guys can share throwing BP or loosen up on the side-line. You decide.

Tomorrow's Friday, so we'll have a team meeting in the morning, make sure they don't have any housing issues, they got all their gear, that sort of stuff. Then we'll have them come back at five again and have a little intra-squad game to sharpen everyone up. Maybe you can throw some on the sidelines, too."

"Me? I can throw? Why, did you talk to Doc? What did he say?"

"He says you're doing fine in therapy. No pain, right?"

"Right."

"OK then, let's see how it feels throwing a baseball around some. Just take it easy. You know the routine. By the way, Kenny said he wanted to open the park for the fans tomorrow afternoon so they can watch us scrimmage. There's going to be a big article in the paper Saturday with all our pictures, plus bios of us coaches, the players, and a recap of all the stuff going on this weekend. It's a big deal. Minor league baseball is important to this town. We always need to put out the right image and keep promoting ourselves to the fine citizens of Rome."

"I understand. I'm seeing a whole different side to things from this angle as opposed to when I was just worrying about playing."

Jamey laughed. "Right. Now we get to worry about all the administrative and marketing stuff. Plus make sure all our kids are concentrating on baseball and trying to make the show."

After Jamey and Brett met with Kenny to go over plans for the opening weekend, Brett had some free time before getting back to the park to meet the team. He found a sunny location in the grandstand along first base and sat down to make several important phone calls. The first would be to his mother to let her know his new address and that he was doing fine.

"Yes, Mom, Rome seems like a real nice town. They have really supported our teams in the past according to Jamey. We're hoping this year won't be any different."

"That's wonderful, Brett. How is your shoulder doing?" He had told her a little, but not all, about his last spring training outing. As far as she knew, the team wanted him to rest it for a few weeks.

"Pretty good, Mom. I'm going to start throwing again, just take it easy and see how it goes. Of course, my most important job now is to keep our young pitchers in line. They have some talent, but Mom, they're just kids, nineteen or twenty years old most of them."

"And just like you were at that age, too, I'm sure. Coaching those boys is a big responsibility, Brett. I know the Braves chose you for a reason."

Brett's next call was to his insurance company, who gave him the necessary instructions for getting the claim filed and repairs completed. Brett pulled the Back Creek Church bulletin out of his pocket and dialed the number written on its front page. Jenny's voice answered.

"Hi, you've reached Jenny's cell phone. Leave me your number and I'll call you right back."

"Uh, hi, Jenny. This is Brett Davies. We met this morning when... I mean I'm the guy that ran into...well, you know. Anyway, I talked to my insurance company. They do need two estimates. If you can get those to me right away, I can fax them to their office. We should get approved to have the repairs started within twenty-four hours. Thanks. Call me. Bye." Brett hung up the phone. *Why was that so nerve wracking? She does have a nice voice, though.*

Brett looked at his watch and saw that he still had two hours before needing to be back at the park for the first practice. On a hunch, he grabbed the Back Creek bulletin and located the church on his city map. It wasn't that far from the park. *Everything is starting to look like a ten- minute drive in this town. Not bad. Just like Albemarle.*

For once, Brett had no trouble finding his destination. He was soon pulling into the parking lot of the Back Creek United Methodist Church. There were several brick buildings, all older but well maintained. The sanctuary with a tall white steeple was nearest the street. It was connected by a long one-story structure that appeared to be offices and meeting rooms to a larger building with a sign, *Back Creek Community Center*, above the entryway. Brett noticed two cars parked near the Center and decided to drive down to that building. He was hoping to find someone who could tell him where Jenny was, or better yet, maybe she was there. Getting out of his car, he walked to the front doors, and found they were open. No one was in the lobby area or at the reception desk. He peered down one hallway marked Church Staff Offices but saw no activity. Another hallway apparently led to their Fellowship Room. Brett thought he heard voices and metal clanging together, so he headed in that direction. Entering the large, dimly lit room he saw two figures moving chairs and tables around, probably setting up for a function later that evening. The taller one saw Brett first.

"Hello, young man. May I help you?" The speaker wore glasses, appeared to be in his mid-forties, and sported a faded Braves ball cap on his head. As he approached, Brett saw that they were about the same height, but the older man was probably thirty pounds heavier. He removed the ball cap and grabbed a towel to wipe the sweat off his face. Brett could see what little hair the fellow had left was starting to turn gray.

"Yes sir. Thank you. I was hoping to find one of your staff members here. Jenny is her first name. I never got her last name."

"You must mean Jenny Lynnville; she's one of our youth coordinators." The big man paused and looked Brett over. "Why do you need to see Jenny?"

Time for an explanation. "Well, sir, my name is Brett Davies. I guess you could say I met Jenny this morning."

The other person entered the conversation. Brett could see he was a young boy, probably eleven or twelve years old.

"Hey, Dad, that's the Braves baseball player Miss Jenny was telling us about this morning."

"I think you're right, Justin." The man turned back to Brett and smiled. "If that's how you introduced yourself to our Miss Jenny, you must have had quite a conversation."

"Yes, sir. I think you could say that's a fair statement."

"I can only imagine. Anyway, Jenny told me all about it. I appreciate that you are going to have your insurance company take care of the damage to our van. Our church budget is tight enough. We don't need to have those kinds of problems." He held out his hand.

"Let me introduce myself. I'm Theodore Fisherman, the senior pastor here at Back Creek. This is my son, Justin. He'll turn twelve later this summer. He likes to think he's a ball player, too."

Brett shook the minister's hand and nodded at Justin.

The youngster spoke up again. "Jenny says you probably know Chuck Killian. Is that true? Can you get him to come up here and talk to our youth group? That would be super!"

"Easy, Justin, we've just met this young man. Like I said, Brett, my boy's a big baseball fan."

"You all must be coming to our first game Saturday night. Jenny said there were quite a few youths and adults planning to be there. She also mentioned another church leader, a Dr. Jake."

"That's true, Brett. You see..."

"He's talking about you, Dad."

"Yes, Justin, let me explain to Brett. My first name is Jacob, but everyone calls me Dr. Jake. You know, like Doctor J, the basketball star. Anyway, that's who I wanted to be like as a kid, but an amazing lack of jumping ability kept me from realizing my dreams." The minister laughed at his own joke and turned to continue setting up chairs and tables. "Jenny works at one of the banks in town during the week, Three Rivers S&L. She is here on Wednesday nights for our mid-week meal and youth Bible study. Then, of course, on the weekends there are all kinds of things going on with the kids, Youth Sunday School, sports programs, planning and fund raising for mission trips. We go see the Rome Braves play several times a year. Plus, we always go to Atlanta for a big league game at least once each summer. So yes, we are a small church, but there is lots to do for all age groups including our youth." He paused and appeared to be deep in thought. "Take our Little League baseball team that Justin plays on, for example. You know we can always use more help."

"So, I've heard."

Dr. Jake stopped setting up and looked over at Brett one last time. "Jenny's many things for us, son. A good recruiter, for sure."

"Yes sir. I could tell that."

Brett walked back out to his car and headed for the ballpark. It had been a long adventurous day, and there was still a lot to do. His mind kept drifting back to Jenny. *Enough of that. Time to get ready for baseball.* The season opener and the official start of Brett Davies' professional coaching career would begin in forty-eight hours.

12

FIRST GAME

Opening night was a beautiful evening for the Rome Braves. The early 6:00 p.m. start ensured that the temperature would stay in the seventies for most of the game. The skies were clear blue, and the winds calm, a perfect night for baseball. Brett was out on the field early to do some running and long tosses. He was working carefully to test the damaged tendon and rebuild his shoulder and arm strength. This was the third straight day he had thrown a baseball since coming off the mound in the exhibition game almost a month earlier. So far, everything felt fine.

Brett looked around the stands as he threw in the outfield with one of his pitchers. The seats were filling up early. It appeared that the full house Rome GM Kiser had predicted was going to be a reality. Coupling opening night with discount tickets for kids guaranteed lots of noise and concession stand activity. The Braves were counting on a good showing in their first game. They needed all those parents and kids back, again and again during the summer.

Brett didn't see Jenny or any of the Back Creek Church crowd, but figured they would get there soon enough. He finished his throwing and trotted back in toward the dugout to put on a dry shirt. The game would be starting in thirty minutes, and he needed to get down to the bullpen to watch over starting pitcher, Scott Buchanan, as he began his warmups. Buchanan was considered one of the Braves' top prospects. He was a hard throwing right hander who needed to develop a curve ball, plus learn to throw strikes. Morey and Schulz, along with Jamey, had made it clear during spring training that they expected their new pitching coach, Brett Davies, to help the young star accomplish his dreams. A loud familiar voice from the stands reached Brett before he got to the dugout.

"Hey kids, look at the player running across the infield. That's Brett Davies, the Braves pitching coach. Everybody say, "Hi, Mr. Brett."

A chorus of young voices boomed, "Hi, Mr. Brett."

Brett didn't need to look up. *I think Jenny might be here.* Glancing up into the stands he first saw Dr. Jake in a section just down the line from their dugout and about fifteen rows up. He was surrounded by kids of all sizes wearing Braves baseball hats. Then Jenny stood up.

"Wave to Mr. Brett, kids."

Twenty little hands waved to their new Braves hero. Brett caught Jenny's eye. He smiled and tipped his cap to his Back Creek admirers, then disappeared into the safety of the dugout.

"What the heck was that all about?"

"Apparently, I have a fan club, Mr. Skiles. All of us stars have one you know."

"We haven't played our first game yet. How in the world did you accomplish that?"

Brett smiled. "Remember about that little 'run in' I had the other day? That was with the Back Creek United Methodist Church van. The church just happens to have about twenty kids and adults up there in Section 7. They want me to help coach their youth teams, maybe put on a clinic with some of our guys as well. I told them to I'd do what I could."

"Well, I guess so, Brett. Just don't forget your day job, OK?" Jamey grew serious. "And that starts tonight, keeping Buchanan focused. The big club is counting on him developing and moving into the Atlanta rotation in a couple years."

"I know, Jamey. Morey and everyone made that real clear. Let me get on a clean shirt, and then I'm headed to the bullpen."

The Braves were opening the season with a two-game series against the Charleston Crawdads. Their Sunday game was starting early so the team could leave later that afternoon for the bus ride to Greensboro and the beginning of a four-day swing through the Carolinas. Rome was scheduled to play fourteen games in the first fifteen days of the season. Jamey and Brett had talked at length about making sure their young squad got off to a good start and remained focused on the task at hand. At this stage of their ballclub's development, the mental aspects would become every bit as important as the physical. Both coaches had seen way too many talented teammates with big league ability who could never handle the long road trips, hostile crowds, and lousy motels and food that came with life in the minor leagues.

Brett reached the bullpen just as Buchanan finished his stretching and began throwing to his catcher, Jerry Penny. The game was starting in twenty minutes. *Everything is on schedule.* It was important that the first game go as planned. Brett wanted all of his pitchers on the same routine so they would know exactly how to prepare, depending on their role as a starter or reliever.

The young righty finished his warmups. They began the long walk together from the bullpen to the Braves dugout.

"You're looking good, Scott. Nice and smooth. You feel OK? Kind of nervous?"

"Yeah, Coach, I admit I've got some butterflies. But I'm fine. Jerry was my catcher last year in the rookie league, so we know each other."

"Sounds good. I'd be worried if you weren't nervous. Just go out there and remember it's still a game. Have some fun, OK?"

"Will do, Coach, will do."

They reached the dugout, and Brett once again heard the cheers of his Back Creek fans. Glancing up into the stands, he saw Jenny smiling and waving to him. The Braves pitching coach tipped his hat once more and stepped down into the dugout. *She sure does have a nice smile.*

For the first game of the season, both young teams were

starting off playing excellent baseball. Brett's only "action" of the night came in the top of the fifth when, with the score tied at 2-2, he went out to the mound to talk to his young pitcher. Buchanan had gotten the first batter of the inning to pop up, but then lost his control and walked the next two Crawdads on eight consecutive pitches.

"Listen, Scott, this is what we've gone over many times before. Take a deep breath, get focused, and let's get out of this little jam." Brett turned to the catcher Penny, who had joined the meeting. "Jerry, just call for the fastball, move it in and out, but keep it down. We need a ground ball right now for a double play."

Buchanan and Penny nodded their agreement. Brett turned to trot back to the dugout. Once more loud cheers came from his Back Creek fan club, but this time he paid no attention as he needed to confer with his manager. "He seems OK, Jamey. He's only thrown fifty pitches so far. He can't be tired. Let's see if he's strong enough mentally to get his rhythm back."

It did not take long for Brett's hopes to be rewarded. Buchanan seemed to be throwing harder than ever, quickly jumping ahead to a one ball, two strike count on the overmatched batter. The next pitch was fired low and on the inside corner. The Crawdads hitter slapped at it, rolling an easy grounder to Braves shortstop, Doug Raymond. Raymond fielded the ball smoothly and turned the soft hit into an inning ending "6-4-3" double play.

The Braves bats came alive in their half of the seventh, getting three runs, including the first home run of the season by their highly rated first baseman, Marv Blanton. Buchanan had pitched a solid game to that point, and Brett told his young hurler that his night was through.

"Good job, Scott. Time for our bullpen to finish this off."

Once again Brett's strategy was rewarded as he got a strong relief performance by one of his "older" players, Maury Brines, a Clemson graduate. Brines allowed only one hit and no runs in his two innings of work. Rome wins 5 to 2.

It was a happy Braves clubhouse after the game. Even though

they had a long five-month season ahead of them, their first victory had made the young professionals even more confident of future success. Jamey and Brett felt the same way but knew full well they were responsible for keeping their team on the right track. There would be many ups and downs and, unfortunately, numerous distractions as well. It was their job to mold these kids who were playing a man's game into major leaguers. Some would make it. Others would drop off. But not because Jamey and Brett hadn't done their job and given their team all they had.

Brett showered and dressed, suddenly mindful of how hungry he was. *Gotta find a good place to eat.* Jamey's family was with him for the summer, so he was going home for dinner. Brett was on his own. Walking out to the parking lot he was surprised to see several fans still hanging around. Then he saw the Back Creek Church van with its dented bumper and rear doors, but still drivable.

"Hey kids, there's Mr. Brett. Go give him a big cheer and congratulations for his first win." It was Jenny, of course. Brett was quickly engulfed by a flock of happy, very loud youngsters.

Good job, Coach.

We're glad you won, Mr. Brett.

Jenny said you're going to coach our team, too. Is that true?

Brett was busy handing out high fives to his fan club, accepting their hugs and pats on the back. He didn't know what to say but tried anyway.

"Thanks for coming out tonight, guys. Our team really appreciates your cheering for us." He saw Jenny and Dr. Jake along with another couple standing outside his little circle of admirers. Jenny was laughing and pointing at him.

"How about it, Brett? Remember, you owe us one."

"Well guys, I sure would like to help some if I can. I don't know. I mean, when do you practice? When are your games?"

Dr. Jake walked over to where Brett was standing. "Don't worry about those details, Brett. Just knowing you'll be able to help us when your Braves' schedule allows is good enough. Tell you what, why don't you join us for church tomorrow morning? You can meet our other coaches and get a copy of the schedule. Then we'll just go from there. OK?"

"I guess so. I need to be back here at the stadium by 11:30, so I don't know if that will work or not."

Jenny jumped back into the conversation. "No problem, Brett. Sunday School is at nine. You can help me with our youth classes, and our worship service starts at 10:15. You'll be at the park right on time."

Youth Sunday School? What do I know about teaching Sunday School? "All right Jenny, you win. I've never taught Sunday school before, but I guess I'm trainable."

With that, the Brett Davies fan club let out another big cheer. Dr. Jake began rounding them up. "Come on, kids. It's getting late. Those that rode in the van with Jenny and me, get in. The rest of you are riding back with Dave and Jana in their car."

Brett walked over to the van with the preacher and Jenny. "You know I'm doing all this for you guys, which is fine." He winked at Dr. Jake. "But Jenny, I think you could help me out a little bit, too." She gave him a puzzled look and waited for Brett to continue. "You see, it's been a long time since I had lunch and right now I am very hungry. My problem is I don't know any good restaurants in this town. But I bet you do. Why don't you come with me, and we'll go get something to eat?"

Giggles from inside the van, "Jenny's got a boy-friend," were quickly stopped. "Hush, kids."

She glanced at Dr. Jake, who smiled and said nothing, and then she turned back to Brett. "Well, OK. But my car is in the church parking lot. You'll have to take me back there when we're done, all right?"

"Nah, I'm making you walk back." He reached out and grabbed her hand. It felt warm and soft. She held on, and they walked to his car.

"So long, kids. I'll see you in the morning."

"Good night, Miss Jenny. Bye, bye, Mr. Brett!"

Brett opened the passenger door and Jenny hopped in. "Well,

it's good to see Southern manners are still in place these days."

"I don't know about that, Jenny." Brett was surprised that he was not more nervous. "I do know that my mom raised her only child the right way." He dialed in a country station on the car radio and was glad to hear Alan Jackson singing a favorite song. He headed the car out of the Braves parking lot and turned left toward town. Jenny spoke again.

"Don't you think we ought to decide where we're going?"

"Uh, good point. I imagine you've lived here a few days longer that me. You choose."

"OK, then can I assume you like good Southern cooking?"

"You bet. That's what I was raised on"

"All right, then. Turn right up here at the next light. There's a good restaurant about two miles up the road." She paused before continuing. "We really don't know much about each other, do we?"

Brett laughed. "You mean other than the fact that I play baseball and am sometimes a lousy driver? What else could you possibly want to know about me?"

"You let me decide that. I'll start with the questions. Where are you from? You said you were an only child?"

Here we go. "I'm from Albemarle. It's a little town, close to the size of Rome, thirty miles east of Charlotte. And yes, I'm an only child, no brothers or sisters. My mom raised me by herself." He looked over at Jenny. "I never knew my dad."

"What do you mean?"

"Just that. I don't know who my dad is. I never met him. It was just mom and me."

Brett was glad that Jenny moved the questions to a different subject. "OK, so have you ever done anything besides play baseball for the Braves?"

"Sort of. You see I got signed after my junior year in college. I went to UNC-Charlotte. Mom made the Braves agree to pay for my last year of school as long as I made good grades. Anyway, it took me three years during the off season to complete my senior year. I did that, and then got my teaching certificate. For the last three years I've been doing substitute teaching and tutoring at my old high school in Albemarle. And, of course, I help coach the sports teams as well."

"Of course. What do you teach? I mean if you can teach a class of rowdy high school kids, my youth Sunday School class ought to be a piece of cake."

"I guess so. But Jenny, my kids aren't rowdy. I'm lucky, I suppose, but for the most part they pay attention. They all know that I play for the Braves, so right or wrong, I get some respect. I teach math and science, mostly."

"Math and science? Well so much for the dumb jock stereotype."

"That's right, young lady. Shows that you never know, doesn't it? So how about you? Where are you from?"

"We're here, Brett. Turn into the parking lot up there on the right."

Brett read the sign, *Ginger's Good Eats* with the added tag line, *BBQ, fresh veggies and more-Home style country cooking.* "This looks perfect, Jenny."

"I told you. Come on, let's go in."

Ginger's diner was a lot larger inside than Brett expected. And even though it was past 9:00 p.m, it was still crowded on this Saturday night. A long lunch counter with bar stools was in the center of the room, with the kitchen area behind it. An assortment of tables and booths were scattered around the rest of the building. Waitresses were scurrying in every direction as Rome's citizens were digging into heaping plates of food, washing it down with sweet tea.

"Hey, Jenny. How ya' doing, girl?" The young lady appeared to be the hostess.

"I'm doing great, Marie. We took a bunch of our Back Creek kids to the Braves game tonight. First one of the season, and we won, too."

"Super. I didn't realize the ball season had started up again." She looked over at Brett and smiled. "Table for two, I assume."

"Marie, this is my friend, Brett Davies. He just moved to town. In fact, he's one of the Braves coaches."

"Really? Nice to meet you, Mr. Davies."

"You can call me Brett, Marie."

The hostess took them to a booth and handed them their menus and silverware. "Here you go. Be sure to look over the specials. Ginger's cooking up some good stuff tonight." She looked over at Brett once more. "You know, I thought you looked familiar. Wasn't your picture in the paper today with that article on the team?"

Brett blushed. "I don't know. I was told they were running a big article on our team in the sports section with pictures and everything. But I haven't seen the paper. I guess it was in there."

"Gee, Jenny, you're with a celebrity. Nice to have you here in Rome, Brett. You be sure to tell all your players about Ginger's. Breakfast, lunch, and dinner, this is the best place to eat in town by far."

"Don't worry; I'll be sure to tell them."

Brett looked over the large menu, trying to decide what to order. Jenny sat across from him, seeming to talk to everyone who walked by and introducing them all to Brett. Finally, there was a brief lull in the traffic to their booth. "Is it just my imagination or do you really know everyone in this city?"

Jenny laughed and took his hand. "Am I embarrassing you, Brett?"

"Well yeah, you're doing a good job of that, too. But you never answered my question."

"I work at one of the biggest banks in Rome, Brett. And then of course I'm up at Back Creek so our kids are often doing service projects or playing against kids from other churches. I seem to meet a lot of people."

"I guess so."

The waitress came with big jars of sweet tea and a steaming plate of hush puppies. "Did we order these?"

"Nope, we just get 'em... I grew up in Atlanta. Three older brothers. I was my mother's last chance for a little girl, and here I am." She threw her arms triumphantly in the air.

Three older brothers. No wonder she's so tough. "How did you end up in Rome?"

"Lucky, I guess. I've always liked this area. My family has a cabin north of here, close to the North Carolina line. We'd spend a lot of time there in the summer, and Rome was about the half-way point of the trip, a good place to stop. Mom and I would go shopping and Dad and my brothers would go to the game when the Braves were in town. When they got older, they'd go play golf. This is just a real nice small town. I'm so glad to be out of Atlanta."

The waitress returned for their order. Brett went for the large BBQ plate with red slaw and beans. Jenny opted for the smaller plate.

"So, how old are you and your brothers?"

"You shouldn't be asking a lady her age, Brett. But OK, I'm 25. How old are you?"

"I'll be 26 later this summer."

"Really, so I'm with an older man tonight, aren't I?"

"Yeah, but I've got a few good years left. At least I hope so."

"I've got a brother two years older than you. He's the youngest. The other two are in their early thirties."

"And I'll have to deal with them, too?" Brett let out a long sigh. "I wish I'd known that first."

Jenny gave him a sly smile. "At some point in time, Brett, I would say you will for sure have to deal with them. They are very protective of their little sister."

"I can only imagine."

The food arrived and they both dug in, tasting the delicious meat and fixings that were one of Ginger's specialties. Brett thought it was as good as advertised...and the company wasn't bad, either. He had been on a lot of first dates, but something about this one was different...a good different.

Their talk continued as they ate. Jenny had graduated from the University of Georgia four years earlier. She was ecstatic when her first job offer was with the Three Rivers Savings and Loan in Rome.

"I started out as a teller, Brett. But now I'm sort of in charge of customer service. I still work at the counter some, but also help customers with opening up accounts, loan applications when one of the officers is out. It's fun. Lots of different things going on. And of course, I get to meet a lot of people as well." She waved at their waitress. "Let's get the banana pudding, Brett? Ginger makes the world's best banana pudding."

"I don't know about that. My mom's is pretty good, too."

"I'm sure, but you'll like this. Trust me." Their waitress was at the table. "Give us a double dish of banana pudding please, Sally-- and two spoons."

"Two spoons? What about all my 'baseball guy' germs?"

"That's OK. I figure you're clean enough." Jenny was quick, tough to keep up with, Brett thought. But he didn't mind trying.

"Thanks for the vote of confidence."

Once again Ginger's food was just as promised. Brett and Jenny dove into their large bowl of bananas and other sweets, devouring it quickly. Sally brought the check and placed it on Brett's side of the table. Jenny was checking her watch.

"It's past ten, Brett. We've gotta get going. I need to be at the church early tomorrow to get everything ready for the kids. How much do I owe you?"

Brett gave Jenny a mock look of alarm. "Owe me? Why Miss Jenny, don't you remember? I'm the guy that wrecked your church van."

"How can I forget?"

"I doubt you ever will. Let's go."

They got up and headed for the cash register. Two men were in line ahead of them paying their bill. The older one turned as they approached and smiled at Jenny.

"Well, hello dear." His heavy northern accent caught Brett off guard. *This guy's sure not from around here.* "This is a pleasant surprise. How are you, Jenny? I normally only see you at the bank."

'I'm fine, thank you, Mr. Vestuti. We were at the game tonight and stopped in for a late dinner."

Vestuti looked over at Brett. "You're Brett Davies, aren't you, the Braves pitching coach?"

Brett was puzzled that he was already that well known. "Yes sir, I am."

The older man held out his hand to Brett. "I'm Gino Vestuti. I own the Victory Gym here in town. We've got all the equipment you need for a good work out. Free weights, nautilus, treadmills, bikes, plus a sauna and steam room." The man talked quickly. *Like a used car salesman.* "All the serious athletes come to my gym. You should, too. I read the article about you and your arm problems. We can help."

"I didn't realize the newspaper article gave everyone that much information on my history."

"Oh, we know all about you, Brett. Here's my card. Come in and use us for a week. No charge. Then if you decide you want to join, we'll work out a special rate for the summer. OK? And tell your players about us, too. We'll do the same deal with them."

The Braves clubhouse did not have any exercise equipment. It sounded like a good opportunity. One he could use as he continued to strengthen his shoulder and prepare to pitch again. *As long as I don't have to listen to this guy talk all the time.*

"Thanks, we're leaving on a road trip after the game tomorrow, but we'll be back in town late Thursday night. I'll try to come by Friday morning."

"Come on, boss, let's get moving."

Brett got his first look at the other man. He was much younger, probably about Brett's age. From his bulging forearms and thick neck, he was obviously one of Vestuti' s serious weightlifters.

"OK, Arnie, we're leaving. The older man turned again to the young couple. "Nice to see you, Jenny. And I look forward to seeing you next Friday, Brett." The two men turned and walked out the door into the Rome night.

Brett finished paying the bill and took Jenny's hand once more as they headed outside to his car. She was quiet as Brett opened the door for her to get in. When he was settled into the driver's seat, she grabbed his arm before he could start the engine.

"Those two might be my customers at the bank, but that doesn't mean I have to like them." She was speaking in a serious tone now; one Brett had not heard before.

"What do you mean, Jenny? Just because they're from New York or wherever and talk different than you, doesn't make them bad people."

"I know, I know. That's not it. Oh, maybe it is. There's just something about them that makes me feel icky."

"Icky?"

"Yes, icky!" I don't know how else to describe it."

"OK, OK. Can we please change the subject? How do I get you back to the church? I'm new in town, you know."

"Yes, you are new." She was laughing again, and it sounded good to Brett. "And don't start looking down at that stupid map when I'm riding with you. Head back like you're going to the ballpark. I'll tell you when to turn."

"Whatever you say, Boss Lady."

Before long, Jenny had navigated them back to the church. Brett pulled into the parking lot. His headlights shined onto one lone vehicle.

"I take it that's your car."

"Very astute, Mr. Davies. You are correct."

She searched for her keys as Brett pulled along side Jenny's car, a red Honda Civic. Shutting the engine off, he turned the key so country music would continue to play. He wondered what he should do next. Jenny solved that problem.

"Well, thanks for a nice evening, Brett. You won your first game and got to eat at Ginger's. Doesn't get much better than that."

She opened her door and got out. Brett waited as she unlocked her car and started the engine. Jenny rolled her window down, motioning for Brett to do the same.

"Maybe we can do this again sometime."

"Sure. I can't wait to meet some more of your icky friends from the bank."

"Very funny. Sunday School is at nine, Brett, so try to get here by 8:30 at the latest. Our Youth Club meets in the Community Building. The same one where you met Dr. Jake and Justin."

"8:30? Gosh I was hoping we could get started earlier."

She rolled her eyes before responding. "Just be there on time, Brett."

Brett followed her car out of the parking lot and back toward town. He was behind her for a few blocks until Jenny turned down a side street he didn't know, and she disappeared into the darkness. He continued straight while looking for a familiar intersection to lead him toward his little home. There was much to think about. His thoughts turned to baseball, their second game tomorrow, and getting ready for their first road trip. Brett looked at his watch and saw that it was approaching midnight. He would be getting up in less than eight hours, but now was wide awake.

He was relieved that for once his sense of direction was correct, and he was soon pulling into his driveway. Once inside, he turned on the television to Sports Center to find out how Atlanta had done and then went into his bedroom to pack for the trip. With that chore completed, he laid down on the couch to catch the news and try to wind down. He remembered that Dr. Jake said he would be meeting the youth baseball coaches in the morning.

Kids, I'm coaching kids for the Braves and now kids for the church. I hope Jenny appreciates that. He closed his eyes and drifted off to sleep thinking about Jenny.

13

A KID'S GAME

The parking lot at Back Creek Church looked far different on Sunday morning than it had the previous evening. Cars of worshipers who attended the traditional early morning service were being joined by a steady stream of vehicles coming for Sunday School, and the late morning contemporary service. Brett pulled his Explorer into the first available space and headed toward the Community Building, where he hoped to find Jenny.

"Well, good morning, Sunshine. Glad you could finally got here."

"You said 8:30, Miss Lynnville, and that was the exact time of day I got out of my car."

"Yeah, yeah. Help me with these lesson handouts. The kids will start arriving in a few minutes. They can't wait to meet you."

"You mean they already know I'm here?"

"Absolutely. The word spread pretty fast after we left the stadium last night. You can thank Dr. Jake for that."

Brett grimaced. "Great, be sure to remind me to do just that."

The classroom was soon filled with noisy middle school boys and girls. The laughter and teasing continued until Jenny got them quieted and seated in the chairs and sofas that were placed around the room.

"OK, listen up," she ordered as she clapped her hands for attention. "I need to introduce you to a friend of mine who is going to be helping our Building Bridges Youth Baseball program this summer."

"We know who he is, Miss Jenny."

"Yeah, he's Brett Davies. He's with the Rome Braves. I heard he knows *Chuck Killian.*"

"He's a 'special' friend of yours, isn't he Miss Jenny?"

Nervous giggles were silenced by their red-faced teacher.

"All right, so you know Mr. Davies. Great, let's get started."

It did not take long for Brett to realize that his primary job would be whatever Jenny asked him to do. That and keep order in the classroom, which he accomplished with an icy stare at the girls or a hard grip on a young man's shoulders. The hour flew by and before he knew it Jenny was dismissing the class. The kids hugged their teacher and shook her new assistant's hand as they headed out the door to the sanctuary for the

worship service.

"Thanks, Mr. Brett. See you next week."

"Are you going to coach our baseball team?"

"Yeah, coach our team, that'll be cool."

"We'll see guys, we'll see," he protested. "I've already got one team to coach, you know."

"Don't worry, kids," Jenny interrupted. "I'll make sure he'll have the time." She smiled at Brett. "Won't we, Mr. Davies?"

"Yea, Mr. Brett's going to be *our coach.*"

"Thanks a lot, Teach."

"No problem. Come on, Brett, we've only got a few minutes before church starts and our coaches want to meet you."

They walked over to another room in the Center and Brett was introduced to the Back Creek youth baseball coaches. Charles Currier had the nine and ten year olds, Dave Slaterman the eleven and twelve age group, while Frank Higgins had the thirteen and fourteen-year old boys. Higgins spoke first.

"Brett, it would be great to have you help us any way and any amount you can." The other coaches nodded as Jenny beamed. "We know your schedule with the Braves is all over the place. We thought, if it's OK with you, rather than ask you to coach one particular team, you could look at all three schedules. Then you just let us know when you're able to come out for a practice or a game, and we'll all make it work."

"Sounds good, doesn't it, Brett?" Currier interjected.

"I think I can do that," Brett replied. "By the way, does Jenny do all your recruiting? She's very good you know." They all laughed. He was glad to see how easy it was to make her blush.

"Great, Brett. Glad to have you aboard." The coaches were all pleased about their new addition. Higgins handed him a schedule of games and practices for each of the three youth teams.

"All our practices and games are over at Segner Field, Brett. They've got four diamonds. The season starts in two weeks and continues through mid-August when the playoffs are over."

Brett and Jenny thanked the coaches and then headed over to the sanctuary. They got there just as the Praise Team began singing their first song. Guitars and drums gave the service a rock and roll feel that Brett was not used to but pretty sure he would like.

"This is our contemporary service, Brett," Jenny whispered as they found some seats a few rows from the back. "The early service is our traditional with all the organ music, hymns, and robes. This is different but still very meaningful. We have about the same amount of attendance for both services, so it's good to give folks what they want. Anything to get them in the door, you know. Heck, some folks come to both."

"I don't think I could handle two services, Jenny," Brett whispered with a wry smile. "We just had the organ music at my church in Albemarle. I think I could get to like this, though."

"Good." She smiled and grabbed his hand as she began singing along to the words projected on the big screen above the stage. Brett listened and tapped his foot to the beat of the drums. He felt Jenny tugging on his arm as the second song started.

"Come on, sing," she implored.

"I'm not very good," Brett protested. "My talent was in sports. God didn't give me any skills in music"

"Don't be so silly. Nobody's going to hear you anyway. *Sing*," she commanded.

Fortunately for Brett and those around him the second song was soon completed. The director motioned for everyone to take a seat as the music continued with a slower tune called "Give Thanks".

Give thanks with a grateful heart
Give thanks to the Holy one
Give thanks for he's given
Jesus Christ his son

Brett found the melody calming, and his thoughts turned to all he was thankful for. The anger and pain from reinjuring his arm in Florida had led to his coming here to Rome...he looked at Jenny seated next to him...and to be with her today. He reached for her hand, and she moved closer to him.

"I'm glad you're here, Brett," she whispered.

"Me too. It's funny how things work out."

"Yeah, funny."

At 6' 4" and with a commanding voice, Dr. Jake was a motivating speaker. Seldom glancing at his notes, he made liberal use of the big screen behind him with slides and short movie clips. Brett chuckled softly when he read the title of the big man's sermon "Is this Heaven?" He nudged Jenny and pointed to his bulletin.

"Field of Dreams," he said quietly.

"What are you talking about?"

"Just wait. You'll see."

As Brett predicted, early into the sermon Dr. Jake asked the congregation to watch a short movie clip. The famous scene of Kevin Costner being reunited on the magical field with his father as a young baseball player was shown on the screen.

"Is this Heaven?" the father asked the son.

"No, it's Iowa," was Costner's understated answer.

Great stuff. Brett took in the corn field scene again. He couldn't remember how many times he had watched it. *Maybe some day I'll meet my dad on a baseball field.*

The service concluded. Brett and Jenny joined the long line of worshipers leaving the sanctuary. Dr. Jake was there with his wife, Nancy, greeting everyone by name and shaking their hand or exchanging hugs.

"Brett, great to see you here, my boy," he said, winking at Jenny. "Of course, it doesn't appear you had much choice, did you?"

"No sir, it seems I have a lot more to do if I want to work off that car crash."

The minister laughed. "And there is a lot more to do. Here, I want you to meet my wife, Nancy. Nancy, this is Brett Davies. The Rome..."

"I know who he is, Jacob. Coaching the Rome Braves." She smiled and took Brett's hand. "Our son, Justin, is very excited. He says you even know Chuck Killian."

"Yes ma'am, Chuck's a good guy. We go back a long way. I'm pretty sure I can get him here sometime this summer.

"That would be wonderful, Brett. You have a nice day. Good -bye Jenny, thanks so much for all you do."

Brett walked Jenny over to her car.

"When will I see you again, Brett? We have Youth on Wednesday night."

"That's a good question. I'll have to check all my schedules now. We go on the road tomorrow and get back Thursday. Maybe you can come to another game. And I think I can make one or two practices for our youth teams since it looks like they start at 5 p.m. I can help out for a little while before heading over to the stadium." He glanced at his watch. "Hey, I've got to get going. Our game starts in ninety minutes.'

She grabbed his hand. "What, no good-bye kiss?"

"Uh, OK, sure." He bent down as Jenny reached up to him. Her lips were soft. He wanted to remember this moment for a long time.

"That was nice, Brett."

"Yeah, we should do that again some time."

"Very funny."

Their conversation was interrupted by the sound of giggling coming from behind a nearby car.

"Look guys, they're kissing. *Miss Jenny kissed Mr. Brett.*"

"Kids," she grumbled.

"Yes, a real problem that's for sure. Maybe we should run them over with our cars."

He bent down and kissed her again. "That'll give them something to talk about. I gotta go. I'll call you, OK?"

Brett raced over to the Braves' stadium and got out onto the field as the team was starting batting practice.

"Nice of you to be here this afternoon," Jamey greeted him.

"Thanks. I think this is going to be a real busy summer."

And it was. Brett's days in Rome were filled with baseball games, church, youth groups, Sunday School, road trips and ...*lucky me...* Jenny.

He had been throwing easy in the outfield for the first month of the season when Jamey asked him if he felt up to pitching some batting practice.

"Your decision, Brett. Might feel good to get back on the mound for a little bit."

Brett agreed. "You're right, Jamey. My arm feels good. Let me give it a try. Maybe three or four batters."

It felt strange as he stepped up on the mound. It had been almost three months since that cold rainy day in spring training. He started slowly and was pleased that his control was good. He threw to four batters, increasing the speed of the pitches to about two-thirds of what he would consider a full effort. His back and legs were tired when he was finished, but his arm felt fine.

Brett knew he needed to build up his strength. Running in the outfield and tossing batting practice were just two elements of the recovery program he needed. Darnell had taught him a good weight training program that worked all areas of his body, so the next morning he decided to go over to Victory Gym to see what they had to offer. Even though Jenny thought the owners were "icky", he didn't see any harm in taking advantage of Vestuti's free trial. The '" gym"' was really a converted supermarket. As Brett walked around for the first time, it appeared to be equipped with all the weight training and aerobic exercise machines he needed. Vestuti was happy that the Braves pitching coach was there.

"Good to see you, Brett. Make yourself at home. Locker rooms are back over in that corner. Do you need one of our trainers to work with you?"

"No, thanks. I've got a pretty good routine a friend of mine gave me to follow. I'll be fine."

An hour later Brett had completed his workout. Sweat drenched his shirt and his muscles had that "good-tired" feeling. *So far, so good.* He was wiping his face with a towel when Vestuti came over to him "Let me show you our whole operation, Brett. You've just seen a part of what we have. I bet you don't know the scale of the nutrition business we do here. That's really the engine that makes us go."

Vestuti took Brett over to the Nutrition Center, where all kinds of protein shakes and other featured drinks could be put together by the hostess for the Victory customers. The warehouse area at the back of the building was stocked with cases of all brands of powders and liquids.

"We do a big on-line business, Brett. Stock and ship everything from right here. If we don't have it, we can get anything you want." He paused and smile at Brett, "and I do mean anything."

Geez, why'd he have to tell me that?

Brett had enjoyed his workout, but not the company. He was glad to get out of the building. *I think I'll try the Y.*

Brett's routine of coaching, working out, and helping the youth groups continued into the summer. The Rome Braves had gotten off to a hot start. Led by a strong pitching staff including Scott Buchanan, Barry Morris, and Maury Brines, the Braves were helped by the big bats of their slugging first baseman, Marv Blanton, and center fielder Bryce Dimitri. They were tough on defense, too. Penny was proving to be an excellent catcher with a strong arm and a good feel for handling his pitchers. Shortstop Scott Cabaniski, along with second baseman Cecil Jackson, made them a solid team up the middle. The young group had clicked from the first week for Jamey and Brett, and by mid-July the Braves were firmly in second place in the standings. They were only two games behind the Charleston River Dogs.

The Back Creek youth teams were also playing "Braves baseball" in their respective leagues. Each team had a winning record and the players, along with hopeful parents, relatives, and friends, were anticipating the season-ending playoffs.

Brett had worked his schedule to make it to a few of the practices and most of the games for each of the three Back Creek teams. Everyone was excited when he was able to join them, and with Jenny's help, he got to know the names of all his players and their parents. With his Rome Braves schedule it was impossible to attend any weeknight games, but each youth team also played at different times every Saturday. When the Braves were not on the road, he could be there. It had not taken GM Kiser long to realize he could not compete with the popular Rome youth baseball league, so the minor league team always played on Saturday evenings. It made for a long day, but Brett enjoyed every minute of it. He told Jenny he worked as hard after each game, as he did during it, answering parent's questions about their son's ability and '" big league"' future.

"What does he need to work on, Brett?"

"What did you do when you were his age?"

Each Back Creek team had its own Team Mom who coordinated post-game snacks and weekly communications. Jenny was there every Saturday, too helping out wherever she could. These were her youth. The kids liked it when 'Miss Jenny and Mr. Brett' were together, Brett coaching and Jenny leading the cheers.

The church teams always drew great crowds as everyone came out to support their boys. Dr. Jake tried to come to all the games, including the ones Justin played in for the older group. The Building Bridges youth girls were at the games, too, gathered around Jenny, giggling and cheering their favorite guys on. *Just like chicks around their mother.* Brett made it a point before each game to look up in the stands, smile, and wave at Jenny and her girls. They loved it.

When the regular season concluded, the playoffs began. Each

Back Creek team fought hard, but with different results. The 9 and 10 year old Little Braves were eliminated in the second round, but both the 11-12 Chiefs and Justin's 13-14 Back Creek Yankees advanced to the finals. Brett was relieved when he saw that the games would be played back--to-- back and not at the same time.

He picked Jenny up the morning of the championship games and they headed over to Segner Field. Brett joined Coach Slaterman on the field and watched the youngsters begin their warm-ups.

"How do they look to you, Dave?"

The coach laughed. "They're a lot calmer than me, Brett, that's for sure. I could hardly sleep last night. And this isn't even the big leagues."

"Maybe not, but it is for these kids." He glanced over to the stands. "And it sure is for all of them, too."

"Yeah, lucky I've got a good wife. Jana keeps me pretty level. She doesn't let this get too big for our son, Denny, either. I told him he was pitching today, and he just said, 'OK, Dad.' Just like that, no big deal."

"He'll do fine, Dave. Don't worry, I'll watch him," Brett assured the nervous coach and father.

The game got under way, and the Back Creek Chiefs quickly found themselves behind 2-0 in the second inning. Their opponent, the Rome Lumber Royals, was threatening to add to the score when two consecutive errors by the Chiefs defense put runners on first and third, with only one out.

Brett walked out to the mound to talk to his pitcher as the Chiefs' catcher and infielders gathered around, arguing about their sloppy play.

"Come on, guys. We got to stop making those stupid errors," said first baseman Stephen Ross.

"Don't call me stupid. I wasn't trying to miss the ball," complained shortstop Nate Matthews.

Brett got to the huddle. He bent down, looking each of his players in the eye.

"*Hey guys, stop it. No more arguing.* Remember what we've

talked about all season. Next play. Forget about those errors. That's gone, done, over. What are we going to do now? That's what we gotta figure out."

"Get a double play, Coach Brett?" offered the little third baseman, Bobby Devaney.

"Yeah, a double play. Perfect. That's what we need, right guys? Denny, I need you to throw your double-play pitch. OK?"

Denny smiled as freckles danced on his face. "Sure Coach, my double-play pitch coming up."

Brett walked back to the dugout and was met by Slaterman.

"What was that all about?"

"Well, it seems they were acting like kids. I needed to get their minds right."

"So, what do we do now, Brett?"

"Well, it's pretty simple, really. We need a double play, so I told Denny to throw his double-play pitch."

"Double- play pitch. What's that?"

"Darned if I know, but I sure hope we find out soon."

The game resumed. Denny looked into his catcher for the sign, nodded his head, and took his stretch. He checked both runners, then wheeled and fired a fast ball to the inside part of the plate. The Royals right-handed batter timed it perfectly and smashed a line drive down the third base line.

"Oh no," Brett moaned.

But Bobby, who was guarding the line, dove to his right, stretching his glove hand out across his body. The line shot stuck in the webbing of the little man's mitt. Bobby stumbled to his feet and dove to the third base bag, tagging it a split second before the surprised base runner could return. *Double play.*

The Chiefs raced to their dugout, pounding each other on the back, and exchanging high fives.

"OK, boys," Coach Dave told his excited team, "You've just proven to Coach Brett and me you can do anything. Now it's time to get some runs to win this game."

And that's what the Back Creek Chiefs did. Bobby's miraculous double play had changed the momentum to their favor. They pounded out consecutive base hits, scoring four runs in the third inning and five more in the fifth. The Royals were deflated. When Denny got their last batter to pop up for the final out, it was fitting that Bobby made the catch. *Chiefs win the championship, 9-2.*

The team celebration went from the field, where they received their winner's trophy, to the parking lot where they were joined by happy parents and fans. Brett could only stay a few minutes as the championship game for the older age group was getting ready to start.

Jenny ran up and gave him a big hug and kiss. "What a game, Brett. I'm so thrilled for our kids."

"I know, I know. I'm already exhausted -- and we've got another one getting ready to start. Plus, I think there's something going on over at the Braves' stadium tonight. What a way to make a living."

"Come on Brett, my boy. Let's go." Dr. Jake grabbed him by the arm. "I hate to break this up, Jenny, but we've got to get ready for another game. Back Creek needs one more victory today."

"I'll be there, and I'll bring everybody with me," she promised.

The Yankees were playing the Etowah Rangers, a team that had already beaten them twice in the regular season. The game was about ready to start when Brett got to the field. Coach Higgins had the boys gathered around him. "Now I know we've lost to these guys, but that's old news," Higgins told them. "We've won five games in a row. We're playing our best baseball of the season right now. Let's jump on 'em early and not let them back up."

Back Creek was the visiting team and batted first. The Etowah pitcher was a hard throwing thirteen year old and the biggest player on the field.

"Anyone get a birth certificate on this kid, Frank?"

"Oh, he's legal, Brett. He was thirteen when the season started and just turned fourteen last month. He goes to school with my son, Reilly. He's a big one though. We need to stand up there at the plate and not back down." Unfortunately, the tall right hander mowed the Yankees down in the first with three quick strike outs.

When the Back Creek team took the field, everyone knew it was going to be a long tough battle.

Joey Stokes was pitching for the Yankees. Brett had worked hard with the youngster all summer and was pleased with his progress. "At least we got our best kid throwing, too, Frank."

"You got that right. This might be a 1-0 kind of game. First team that flinches loses."

Stokes retired the Rangers three up, three down, and the tone of the game had been set. Neither team could break through against the other until the bottom of the sixth, when the Rangers pushed across the first run of the game on a walk and two singles. Stokes recovered to retire the side, but the damage was done. The Yankees hustled in from the field for their last chance in the top of the seventh.

Justin was leading off for Back Creek. Brett took his coaching position along third base and hollered encouragement to the minister's son.

"OK, Justin, now's the time. We need base runners. Look for your pitch."

Brett glanced into the stands and saw that the entire Back Creek crowd was on their feet cheering and clapping their hands, trying to will their team to victory. Dr. Jake had his arms folded; his eyes focused on the field as his son stepped into the batter's box.

The Etowah right hander was still throwing hard, but Justin managed to foul off a couple pitches, and eventually worked his way to a full count. The youngster continued to battle, fouling off two more pitches, before a pitch in the dirt sent him racing to first. He was only the third base runner of the game for Back Creek. Brett signaled for the sacrifice, and Reilly Higgins laid a perfect bunt down the third base line that moved Justin to second. The next Yankee batter connected on a long fly to left, but the Back Creek fans moaned as the Rangers outfielder camped under it to collect the second out of the inning. Justin held at second after the catch. The Yankees pitcher, Joey Stokes, came up to bat with a chance to keep the game going with a base hit.

"*Justin,*" Brett hollered over the crowd's noise, "get a good lead. You're moving on any hit. Watch me. I'll let you know if you're going home."

Stokes worked the count to two balls and a strike. The Rangers' pitcher wound up and fired a hard fastball down the middle of the plate. *Crack.* Joey connected and lined a hard single into right field past the diving second baseman.

"*Come on, Justin,*" Brett was pumping his arms furiously. *He's got to score on this.* Brett waved Justin around third base as the Etowah outfielder scooped up the ball and prepared to throw home. *It's going to be close.* The crowd was going crazy on both sides of the stands. Justin raced toward home plate as the Rangers catcher prepared to receive the long throw from the outfield.

"*Slide, Justin, slide!*" The baseball and runner collided at home plate, disappearing into a cloud of red dust. The umpire hesitated, and then made his call.

"*You're out, out.*"

The Etowah players threw their gloves into the air and raced to the pitcher's mound, piling onto one another in a happy scrum. The Back Creek team and its fans watched the celebration in stunned silence. Young and old tried to hide their disappointment. Brett ran to home plate to check on Justin, who was still lying on the ground.

"Come on Justin, get up. You played a great game. Nothing to be ashamed of." Brett reached down and pulled the youngster to his feet.

"I thought I was safe, Coach. I lost the game for us. I should've run faster." Justin's lower lip was quivering as he spoke. Brett dusted red dirt off Justin's uniform and gave him a big hug.

"Nonsense. You need to remember how hard you all played, never giving up. You've got a lot to be proud of. I know I am."

"And so am I." Dr. Jake had reached the field by now, anxious to check on his son. "This baseball season was the best Back Creek Church has ever had, and you were a big part of it, Justin. I'm proud of you, son."

"Thanks Dad," Justin's eyes started to brighten. "I still wish I'd been safe."

"I know. Life's like that sometimes. Makes you appreciate the wins more, doesn't it, Brett?"

"It sure does."

The preacher turned to Brett and put his hand on the coach's shoulder, "I meant what I said. This has been a wonderful season for our church family, especially for the young boys that you coached. We have so many happy memories and lessons to take away from all this. We're very proud and grateful that you've been a part of all this, son."

The two teams lined up to shake hands and congratulate each other on the great game and sportsmanship that all showed. Jenny was waiting for Brett in the parking lot after the Back Creek team received their second place trophy.

"Brett. I don't know how," she sighed, "but that game was wilder than any of them. I feel so sorry for Justin. Do you think he'll ever get over it?"

Brett looked over Jenny's shoulder where Justin and players from both teams were enjoying their snacks. Laughter from the boys, and giggles from the girls who had joined them, meant things were pretty close to normal.

"I think he'll survive somehow, Jenny." He smiled and reached for her hand. "Come on, I've got another game to get to."

14

A MYSTERIOUS STRANGER

That night, the Rome Braves played as hard as their Little League namesakes, pulling out a tough 4-3 win over the Augusta Green Jackets in the bottom of the ninth. It had been a long day for Coach Davies, and the hot shower after the game felt good on his aching body. He had pitched batting practice again that evening, as he had done every other day for the last eight weeks. He was worn out, but his arm and shoulder felt strong. Jamey and Brett were getting dressed when the manager spoke.

"Brett, we're on the home stretch now. Only two more weeks and we're just a game and a half out of first place in our Southern Division."

"Yeah, Jamey, I sure didn't think we'd play this well all summer. Most of these guys have never played more than sixty games in college or the Rookie League. Jumping up to one hundred forty is a big deal physically and emotionally. It's not gonna get any easier. We only have one day off from now till the end of the season."

"You're right about that. Let me ask you something. How do you think our pitching staff is holding up?"

"They're all a little tired, of course. Especially Maury. He's not pitched many innings, but we've had him finish a lot of games for us. He's been a real workhorse, but he could use some help."

"I agree. Good thing, too, 'cause I'm looking at that help right now."

"Who . . . me?"

"Of course, you. Who the heck else am I looking at? Brett, I'm putting you on the active list tomorrow. I'll let you decide when to put Brett Davies into the game."

Brett laughed as he and Jamey walked out of the locker room and to the parking lot. Jenny was waiting for him. "OK, Skip, I'll be sure to talk to our new relief pitcher and make sure he's ready when we need him."

The Braves left Monday morning for Charleston and the first of three games with the Northern Division leading West Virginia Power. They would finish the road trip with two games Thursday and Friday night with the Hagerstown Suns, a farm club of the Washington Nationals. After the Friday game, they would get back on the bus and ride all night back to Rome. They would arrive in time for a Saturday evening start to their next to last home stand. It would be a long trip for the young minor leaguers, all part of "paying their dues". They looked forward to someday playing in the major leagues-- "the Show" -- with its accompanying jet travel, nice hotels, and generous daily meal allowance. The long bus rides would someday be a thing of the past.

Jamey announced to the team in their pre-game meeting that Brett had been activated for the remainder of the season. The applause and shouts of encouragement from his (now) teammates made Brett unusually nervous as he considered once again pitching in a real game.

"Thanks, guys. I appreciate all that." He looked around the room at the smiling faces. "You know, it's not gonna be hard for 'me' to put 'me' in the game," he paused for effect. "But deciding when to take 'me' out of the game? Now, that's going to be tough for Coach Davies." The players laughed and cheered once more.

Reenergized, they headed out to the field to get ready for their first contest with the Power. The game started out as a slug fest, as neither team's pitcher was very effective. Going into the bottom of the seventh, West Virginia had a 14-8 lead. Brett decided his new relief pitcher needed to warm up. *No sense wasting any more arms in this one.*

Walking out to the bullpen from the Braves dugout, he could feel the adrenaline pumping through his body. He began taking his first tosses and checked the action on the field. Brett could see that his pitcher, Thomas Allen, who was drafted out of Duke just two months earlier, was struggling. Three hits and two walks later, the bullpen phone rang. "Tell Jamey I'm ready," Brett yelled. He hurried to get a few more pitches in before heading to the mound.

Jamey was waiting with a big smile on his face as he handed Brett the ball. "One out and bases loaded. Just the way you like it, Brett. Go get 'em."

"Thanks, Jamey. Don't wait too long for this to turn into a disaster.

Jamey gestured at the scoreboard. "16-8, Brett. I think it already has. I'll make sure our pitching coach keep a close eye on you."

"Gee, thanks."

Brett threw his six warm up pitches, checked signs with Penny, and toed the rubber. Jerry asked for an inside fast ball on the right handed hitter, and Brett responded with a precise throw that cut the corner of the plate. Strike one. Two fastballs later, Brett was ahead in the count. One ball and two strikes. *Time for the big curve. Let's find out how strong my shoulder is.* Looking in for the sign, he shook his head till Jerry gave him the one he wanted. Brett took his stretch and fired his sidearm curve at the batter's rib cage. The result was perfect. The young hitter practically dove out of the batter's box just as the ball turned sharply and crossed the outside corner of home plate for a called strike three. Brett continued to work comfortably to the next Power batter, and quickly coaxed an inning-ending pop up to Blanton at first base.

"Nice job, pitch." Jamey patted him on the shoulder as Brett got his warm-up jacket on and took a seat on the bench.

"Thanks, Skip. I felt good out there. Kind of surprised me."

"Yeah, just like riding a bike. Maybe our pitching coach should have put you in sooner."

"Very funny, I still need to get through the eighth inning, you know."

"And maybe the ninth, too. All we have to do is score eight runs in two innings."

Brett got the West Virginia team out in order in the bottom of the eighth, but the Braves batters could not do their part in the ninth inning. The game was over.

"Hey Jenny," Brett was anxious to call her with his good news when he got back to the motel room. "Be sure to check out the box score in the morning paper. You might see a familiar name."

"I will, Brett. That's wonderful, but I'm sorry our guys lost."

"We'll be fine. Four more games before we head home. We can't dwell on this one."

"OK, be safe. I love you."

"I love you more."

"No, you don't."

Brett gave up. "All right, you win. I'll call again soon."

The Braves responded just how Brett and Jamey had hoped, sweeping the next two games from the Power. Buchanan and Morris, who had turned into Brett's best pitching prospects along with Brines, got the wins. Blanton and Penny led the hitting attack, along with a game-winning double from Demitri in the final game. The Braves were off to Hagerstown, and everyone was feeling great.

Brett put himself in to pitch during both games with the Suns and continued his strong performance from his West Virginia debut. Rome and Brett Davies were on a role, winning the two games with the Suns to finish up the long road trip. Brett's stats over a dazzling seven innings of work showed no runs given up, eight strike outs, two hits, and just one walk. It was an excited team that got on the bus for the long ten-hour drive home. They had two games at State Mutual Stadium before heading back on the road Monday. The sound of noisy chatter from the players as the bus started down Interstate 81 was broken by the ring of Jamey's cell phone. The call lasted a few minutes.

"Hey guys, listen up." The skipper waited for the players to settle down before continuing. "That was Kenny on the phone. The River Dogs lost tonight. We're now tied with them for first with only eight games to play -- and the last three are against them. Plus," he continued, "all the rest of our home games are sold out. That's the two this weekend and then the final series against the River Dogs."

The Rome Braves roared their approval as the long ride continued into the night. Brett settled down into his seat, tired but happy. It was the "cool of the evening" again, and he would be seeing Jenny soon. Life was good.

The stands were indeed jammed with Braves fans when the Saturday night game against the Lexington Legends, the Class A farm team of the Houston Astros, got under way. The Back Creek crowd, led by Jenny and Dr. Jake, were in their usual seats. "And we're all coming back tomorrow night too, Brett," Jenny had informed the Braves player/coach before giving him a quick good-bye kiss as they left Ginger's earlier that afternoon. Brett headed to the stadium, and Jenny went back to the church to round up her kids.

The Rome players delivered for the packed house, grinding out a hard fought 6-5 win over the Legends. Outfielder Jimmy Bavista and short stop Scott Cabaniski, along with second basemen Wayne Dickerson, were the hitting stars. Mickey Worner, another young hurler drafted out of Florida, pitched six tough innings. Brett's bullpen held on with Brines getting three quick outs in the ninth for his thirty-fifth save of the season.

After the game, Brett and Jenny joined the Back Creek youth group at the Rome Pizzeria, where Dr. Jake and Nancy were also waiting. The pizzas had already been ordered. Before long, everyone was enjoying the cheesy crust and hot toppings of sausage, pepperoni, and mushrooms. All the kids crowded around the table.

"Will you be pitching tomorrow night, Mr. Brett?"

"Yeah, we'll cheer you on this time."

"Good game, Coach. I sure hope I get to see you pitch tomorrow."

The enthusiasm over the first-place Rome Braves and their new pitching star, Brett Davies, continued the next day at church. Dr.

Jake was preaching about "Onward Christian Soldiers," proclaiming that it was "just like our youth baseball teams and our Rome Braves as they gear up for battle."

"That's a little too much, don't you think, Jenny?" he whispered to her.

"Oh relax, Brett," Jenny hugged his arm. "Dr. Jake always uses sports symbols in his sermons."

"Yeah, I know. But I never feel like I'm 'marching off to war.' I mean, it's a *baseball game.*"

"I know, Brett. But baseball at all levels is very important in this town."

"No kidding."

That night, on a hunch, Brett started the Duke hurler Allen. The right hander responded brilliantly and pitched eight strong innings. The game was tight, as the Braves held on to a 2-1 lead going into the ninth. Brines had come on to start the inning and got the first batter out, but then gave up two quick hits. Brett was already warming up as Jamey walked to the mound. The skipper motioned to the bullpen. Brett was going into the game.

The crowd's cheers were led by the youth of Back Creek Church as Brett trotted to the mound.

Come on, Mr. Brett.

You show 'em.

Throw the double- play pitch, Coach.

Brett was smiling as he took the ball from Jamey's hand. "What are you so happy about?" the manager inquired.

"Oh, nothing. I was just thinking that I'll throw this guy my double play pitch. Then we can all go home and get some sleep."

"Well, I don't know what pitch that is, but I like the idea. Go get 'em, Coach."

There were runners on first and second as Brett took the stretch for his first pitch of the season in front of the home crowd. He fired a low strike across the knees.

Way to go, Coach Brett.

Two more. You can do it.

The excited crowd was on their feet, cheering their heroes to victory. Taking a deep breath, Brett looked in for the sign from his catcher and nodded at the curve ball. He decided to throw this one over the top so it would break straight down. *Maybe he'll knock it into the ground to Jackson or Cabaniski, and I'll get out of this.* Brett spun the ball up to the plate, snapping it off his fingers with all the force he could give it. But it wasn't enough. The Legends batter swung at the hanging curve and smashed a line drive up the middle... straight at Brett. Brett had finished his follow-through and reacted instinctively, throwing his glove up in front of his face. The ball rocketed into the mitt, the force knocking him to the ground. Out of the corner of his eye, Brett caught Blanton heading back to cover first base. While still on his knees, Brett fired a strike to Marvin who stepped on the bag a split second before the retreating Lexington base runner. *Double play. Braves win.*

Brett scrambled to his feet as his happy teammates came from all sides to congratulate him. The Back Creek group was waiting behind the dugout. Brett was their very own hero of the game.

Great game, Brett.

Yeah, that ending was awesome.

Way to throw the double play pitch, Coach.

Brett took his time talking to as many kids and parents as he could. Everyone was in a great mood, wishing him continued success for the rest of the season. But it was Sunday night, and school was back in session. Too soon for all, they had to break up their victory party and head home...even Jenny.

"That was so exciting, Brett. I've never seen you pitch before. I guess you weren't lying to me. You really can do that, can't you? But you need to be more careful, young man, and not let them hit the ball at you so hard."

"That was all part of my master plan. It worked, didn't it?"

"I don't care. Don't scare me like that. OK?"

"Yes, ma'am. I'll do just as you ordered."

Jenny rolled her eyes, pretending to be angry. She leaned over the railing for a kiss. It would be Thursday before they saw each other again. "Is this what the life of a baseball wife is like, Brett? Saying goodbye all the time?'

"I wouldn't know, Jen. I've never been a baseball wife."

"Very funny," she sniffed.

They embraced for the last time. Jenny had tears in her eyes as she turned to leave the stadium to get to her car. The parking lot was nearly deserted, as was the Braves' stadium that had earlier been packed with screaming fans. Brett stepped down into the dugout and started the long walk down the hallway to the locker room.

"I'm proud of you, Son."

The voice startled Brett. He thought it came from behind him, but no one was there. Racing back to the dugout, he jumped out onto the field searching the stands. There were only a few ushers and members of the ground crew cleaning up the stands. *Who was that? Someone I should know? A stranger?* He shook his head as he ran back into the dugout, down the hallway, and out the door that led to the parking lot. It was empty except for a couple vehicles he recognized as belonging to some of the Back Creek parents. In the distance the church van was pulling out of the lot. Jenny and Dr. Jake followed in their cars.

He went back to the locker room and into the coach's office. Jamey was sitting at his desk, looking over the box score from the game. "Where you been, Brett? Talking to your adoring fans?" Jamey stopped and looked at his friend. "Man, you're pale as a ghost. What's the matter? That line drive scare you worse than I thought?"

"Nah, nothing like that. It's just that I heard someone."

"Well, I guess so. We had five thousand fans here tonight."

Brett sighed. "Not that. I mean, I was walking down the hallway. There wasn't anyone around, but I thought I heard someone talking to me."

"Really? So who was it? What did they say?"

"I don't know," Brett paused. He was tired. It had been another long day of many long days in this baseball season. "Maybe it was no one."

But maybe it was.

15

DISCOVERY

The Rome Braves bus was scheduled to leave the stadium Monday morning for the start of the team's last road trip of the season. It would be a short one. The Braves had two games in Greensboro and a Wednesday afternoon make-up contest in Kannapolis before heading back home. Thursday would be a much needed day off. The team would be able to rest and prepare for the final three games of the year which would start Friday night against the Charleston River Dogs. The Friday game would also include a visit from the Atlanta Braves hitting star, Chuck Killian, who would entertain the fans with a pre-game home run hitting contest ...with Brett pitching, of course... and an autograph session.

Brett took his usual seat opposite Jamey at the front of the bus and tried to settle in for the six-hour ride to Greensboro. His mind was racing though, his thoughts far from the ballgames to be played. That voice had to be his dad. *'I'm proud of you, Son.'* It sounded so familiar. He wondered how long he had been watched. Brett was excited and troubled at the same time, but he decided not to tell Jenny. At least not until he had a chance to figure things out. He tried to block out the noise from his players' conversations, card games, and arguments. He had only told Jamey about the "voice". His skipper could sense something was wrong.

"What's up, Brett? You look like you've got a lot going on inside that brain of yours."

"I'm sorry, Jamey. Yeah, I guess. You know, end of season, what's going to happen next. There's lots of stuff to think about." And even more he didn't want to bring up.

"Brett, you've got nothing to worry about. You're doing a great job with this pitching staff. Believe me, Morey knows it, the whole organization does. Heck, I'd like nothing better than to go to spring training next year and have you and I together again. Maybe get promoted to our AA team down in Jackson."

"Yeah, Mississippi in the summertime. A real garden spot, I'm sure. Sign me up for that."

Jamey smiled as the mood of his player/coach started to lighten. "Say what you want now, Brett. But that gets us one step closer to the bigs. You know what I mean?"

Brett laughed at his friend. "I know, Jamey, I know. Someday we'll be sitting in our rocking chairs reminiscing about the wonderful, cool summer nights we spent together in Jackson, Mississippi. I can't wait."

"Neither can I, Brett. Neither can I."

Brett closed his eyes to rest, but still could not get the mysterious voice out of his mind. His thoughts drifted to Jenny, Dr. Jake, and the Back Creek baseball teams. The kids had a wonderful season. Brett received lots of thanks and congratulations from the other coaches and parents for his contribution. Dr. Jake was pleased with how Brett had helped Justin improve as a player. It was strange how it had all worked out so well. If he hadn't tweaked his shoulder in spring training, he never would have gotten the chance to coach in Rome . . . or meet Jenny. He was a lucky man.

The bus rolled on down the highway while Brett's mind continued to rush over the summer activities, leading up to the mysterious stranger. *But where have I heard that voice?* Brett dozed off dreaming of big games on the mound and voices from the grandstand. He didn't know how long he had been asleep or where they were when he was jarred awake. *Could it be? How can I know for sure? What should I do now?* He thought for a few minutes, trying to control his trembling body. He turned to Jamey.

"Skip, I need a favor." He was starting to sweat.

"Sure, Brett, what's up?"

"Well, I haven't been home since February. We've got an off day Thursday after our game in Kannapolis, and Albemarle is less than an hour away. I can rent a car in Kannapolis, drive down to Albemarle, and spend the day with my mom. I can be back in Rome Friday in plenty of time to meet up with Chuck and get ready for our game with Charleston."

"Sounds like a plan, Brett. Let me call Beth back in our office and see if she can get you a good deal on a rental car."

"That would be great, Jamey. Thanks a lot."

Brett settled into his seat and tried to relax. There was only one way to put the missing pieces of his life together, and they were inside a trunk in Albemarle.

The Braves split their two games in Greensboro. They won the first, 6-3, but lost the Tuesday night game, 15-4, when Brett's bullpen ran out of gas. Brett pitched the eighth inning, and it was the only time all night the Grasshoppers were shut down without a run or hit.

"Maybe you should have pitched the whole game," Jamey told his coach after the game with just a hint of sarcasm.

"I was going out to the mound almost every inning anyway, Jamey. I guess I should have taken my glove with me and saved myself a whole lot of walking." They both laughed. It was a winner's laugh. The Braves were still tied for first place with Charleston.

"I think you're right Brett. Hey, I got a call from Beth, and she's got a car waiting for you in Kannapolis. We can pick it up on the way to the park tomorrow morning."

The team was already on the bus when Brett and Jamey left the stadium. It had been a long game and it was almost midnight. They would stay in Greensboro and make the one-hour drive to Kannapolis in the morning for the noon start of their make up game. It would be a long day, but the Braves would be back in Rome Wednesday night to enjoy their day off on Thursday. The two coaches were about to get on the bus when the ringing of Jamey's cell phone startled both of them.

"It's Kiser." Jamey glanced at Brett with a look of concern sweeping over his face. "What could Kenny want? I already talked to him tonight right after our game was over." He hit the talk button. "Yeah, Kenny. What's up?"

Brett watched as Skiles' face grew more serious. "Are you sure? All three of them?"

More listening.

"What do you want us to do? OK. OK. We'll talk to them right now. We haven't left the stadium yet." The skipper hung up the phone. "This isn't good, Brett."

"What the heck's going on, Jamey?"

"The league office just called Kenny a few minutes ago. Three of our guys failed their drug tests. They tested positive for *steroids*."

"What? Who?" Brett felt a familiar knot in his stomach. *Not again. Not these guys.*

"Wayne and Bryce were two of them, Brett . . . and so was Scott Buchanan."

Brett's heart sunk. It was bad enough that any of them got mixed up in steroids. But Scott? Brett had invested so much time in the young pitching star and now . . . "It's just like before. I never saw it coming."

Jamey ignored Brett's comments. "We've got to get them off the bus now and tell them. They're suspended for the rest of the season. The league doesn't want them talking to anybody. They'll be interviewed by one of the minor league drug enforcement guys when we get back to Rome. Probably find out the rest of their punishment then."

Brett nodded. "OK. I'll go get them." He walked over to the bus and climbed on board. "*Wayne, Bryce, Scott.* Skip and I need to see you outside right now. Hurry up."

The puzzled players jumped out of their seats, scrambled down the stairs, and hustled over to where Jamey and Brett were standing. Two dozen eyes were staring out the bus window as the scene unfolded in the parking lot. Jamey spoke first.

"Guys, I'm not going to make your day. I just got off the phone with our GM. Mr. Kiser received a phone call about thirty minutes ago from the league office informing us that each of you failed your last drug tests. *"Steroids. You idiots have been taking steroids."* He stopped, trying to compose himself. Brett watched for reactions from each of the players. Their heads were down, unable to face the two men in front of them. After a long uncomfortable moment of silence, the skipper continued.

"I don't know how this will ultimately end up. I will tell you what I do know. First, each of you is suspended for the rest of the season. Second, each of you will be interviewed by a minor league official on Thursday back in Rome. In the meantime, you are not to talk to anybody, and I do mean anybody, about this. That means team-mates, parents, girlfriends, no one. Only Coach Davies, me, and Mr. Kiser, that's it. You'll know more about your punishment and what you can and can't do after your interview on Thursday."

Brett couldn't stay silent any longer. "Do any of you have any-thing to say? Can you tell me why you did something so stupid? You knew you'd get caught, didn't you?"

Bryce and Wayne just shook their heads and remained quiet. Scott spoke first. "I'm sorry, Coach," he blurted, "I really am. It's just that my arm was hurting. I didn't feel like I had any pop, and I knew the team needed me. Anyway, he said this stuff would help me get stronger."

"He? Who's he?"

"You know him, Vestuti, the owner of Victory Gym. We've been working out there all summer. He claimed it would be masked, un-detectable. I guess it wasn't." Scott stopped and dropped his head, his once promising future now possibly gone forever.

Vestuti, my gosh, Jenny was right about them all along.

Brett felt like he was back in Principal Harland's office. "You guys have committed a very serious offense. Now you must face the consequences. I hope each of you will handle what-ever hap-pens like a man, and never go down this road again." Brett glanced over to Jamey, and then back to the three players. "Let's get back on the bus."

"Yes, sir," they responded. There was nothing more to say.

The short ride back to the motel was quiet. Brett and Jamey were sharing a room, but each was too deep in thought to talk much about the steroid issue. Brett wanted to tell Jenny what had happened but knew he couldn't. Her suspicions about Vestuti were correct.

The ride down to Kannapolis the next morning was uneventful. They stopped at the rental company, so Brett could pick up his car and then follow the team bus to the stadium. The Braves were able to defeat the Intimidators, 3-2, in a tight well played ball game. "A great way to finish the road trip," Jamey congratulated his troops. "Let's all take advantage of the day off tomorrow, so we can finish the season strong. I want to sweep Charleston three straight." The Rome Braves let out a big whoop and holler proclaiming their excitement for the highly anticipated weekend series.

Brett had not heard any discussion about the troubles of the three teammates. It wasn't Scott's turn to pitch, while Wayne and Bryce were nursing "injuries." *They'll find out soon enough.* Brett needed to move on to another important matter. He loaded up his gear in the rental car and was preparing to leave when he saw Jamey motioning for him.

"Kenny just called. The league will be interviewing them tomorrow afternoon in his office. He doesn't know exactly when this all starts, but I would really like it if you could be there. I think it would help."

"Sure, I understand Skip. Let me know when you find out what time, and I'll be there. None of us knew any of this was going to happen when I planned this little side trip. I'll spend some time with Mom and get back to Rome as soon as I can." *And do some investigating of my own at home, too.*

The fast play and early noon start of the Braves' game with the Intimidators had worked to Brett's advantage with his tight timeline. He checked his watch. *3:30. I should be home by 4:15 and mom gets off at five. That should give me enough time.* Brett said good-bye to Jamey. He jumped in his car, headed south on I-85, then took NC 73 over to his hometown. Soon he was pulling into his driveway. Brett grabbed his bag, found the front door key in its customary hiding place under the flowerpot on the porch, and let himself into the quiet house.

He felt strange. His hands were shaking in nervous anticipation. Brett sat his bag down and headed for the door leading to the attic stairs. *Is this when I find out? Could it be?* Brett kept replaying the voice in his head. *"I'm proud of you, Son."* He turned on the light and headed up the stairs. There would only be a few minutes before his mother got home. He needed to work fast. The big trunk was sitting there surrounded by other boxes that Brett had carried up to the attic just six months earlier. He thought of the Rome Braves, and Jenny, and his mom. He wondered what would happen to the three players who failed their drug tests. What should he do about Vestuti? He sighed. *And will I ever find my dad?*

The attic heat caused him to start sweating, but his mouth was dry. With shaky hands, he opened the trunk and took out his mother's high school yearbook. The envelope with the flower in the plastic bag were still there along with the note. He read it again, *"To Lizzie, all my love"* and stared at the Valentine drawn with the initials *"JF+ ED"* inside the heart. Opening the yearbook, he found his mother's picture in the junior class, Elizabeth Davies "Lizzie". His eyes scanned down the pictures on each page looking for the young man with the initials from the note. There was no match. His heart sank. *Maybe I was wrong. No. He had to go to school with her.* Turning to the senior class, he resumed his search. D, E, F. *William Fanning, James Farlow, Steven Finley.* He stopped and stared at the next color portrait. A young man with blue eyes, long blond hair, and sideburns in the style of the day. *He kind of looks like me.* He read the name and smiled. A sudden calmness came over his entire being. *Jacob Fisherman,* the realization starting to take hold. *JF, Jacob Fisherman, Dr. Jake . . . my dad. But why could he not be with me? Why the distance...why the secrecy?* Tears came to Brett's eyes. They had missed out on so much together. Brett needed answers. He carefully placed the yearbook back in the trunk and turned to go back down the stairs.

"Brett, are you up there?"

He hadn't heard his mother come in." Yeah, Mom, I'll be right down."

She appeared at the foot of the stairs. "What on earth are you doing up in the attic?"

He hurried down the steps and gave her a big hug. "And it's good to see you, too, Mrs. Davies."

"Oh, Brett, of course I'm glad to see you." She gave him a quick kiss on the cheek. "But I still don't know why you were in the attic."

"I think you'll understand, Mom. Come on. Let's sit down. We've got a lot of catching up to do. A bunch of things have happened to me since I left here for spring training, and ninety-nine percent of them are good." They walked to the screened-in porch at the back of the house. It was a warm August evening. Brett turned on the ceiling fan, as Mrs. Davies poured each of them a tall cold glass of sweet tea. "Now, Brett, please tell me what's going on."

Earlier he had told her about Jenny, his Braves team, and coaching the Back Creek baseball teams during his many phone calls home. He decided to start with the voice. "I couldn't shake it, Mom. I just felt like that was my father speaking to me. And I knew I had heard that voice somewhere."

Mrs. Davies looked away for a long moment, then turned back to her son. "When you told me you were going to Rome to coach the Braves team, I thought somehow this might happen. All those events -- hurting your shoulder again, getting a chance to coach, and then it's in Rome. They all happened for a reason, Brett. God knows what He's doing, and I believe He knew it was time."

"So JF on the prom napkin, that's . . ."

"Jacob Fisherman, your father. I think you call him Dr. Jake, don't you, Brett?"

Brett shook his head. "But why couldn't he be here with me, with you? Why all the secrecy all these years?" His voice grew louder as his frustration mounted. "I should have had him here; he's my dad. I don't understand. *It's not fair.*"

Brett's mother started to cry as she faced her son. "I know you don't understand, Brett. It was a horrible time. I was pregnant. We were both so young. Our parents were ashamed and angry with the two of us. Jake's dad was adamant that nothing was going to stop his son from being a minister." She paused to collect herself, before continuing in a soft voice. "I was sent away to a boarding school for my senior year... and to have you. When I came home, I stayed with your grandparents for a while till I could get a job and get my own place. His parents paid all the medical bills and sent money each month to help with other things. But Jake and I weren't allowed to see each other."

"What do you mean? Even after he graduated? I think he did what his parents wanted and chose his career over you and me."

Brett could only listen, as his mother continued. "Yes, I guess we did what our parents asked us. But Jake knew, and I knew, that he wanted to be a minister. Back then, probably still today, there was no way that would happen if the church discovered he had fathered a child out of wedlock. Maybe it was wrong, but I understood it had to be kept a secret. And I wanted to help him realize his dream. Of course, I was hurt at first. Being sent away was awful, and you can imagine the rumors in this small town. But that was a long time ago. I have never hated your father. He promised to help financially. Once he got his own church, he sent a check every month. He never missed one right up to the time you signed with the Braves. And you know he never forgets you on your birthday and at Christmas."

Brett leaned forward and took his mother's hand tightly in his. "It was so strange, Mom. Things all happened so fast. I remembered the yearbook and needed to come home to find out for sure."

She smiled at her son. "Like I said, Brett, it was time."

"But why couldn't I know him when I was growing up? Why all the secrecy? I just don't understand why he couldn't be in my life, in some way, as I was growing up."

"Oh, but he was, Brett. He came back numerous times to watch you play football, basketball, and especially baseball. Your father was quite an athlete, too. I'm sure that's where you got your abilities."

Brett smiled, "I know, Mom."

"Don't hate him, Brett. He loves you very much. I'm sure this summer had to be very strange and exciting for him, too. I think in his own way he was trying to reach out to you. He knows it's time, I'm quite sure."

"Have you talked to him about me?"

"Just once. I called him the day you told me you were going to Rome. Of course, he was very excited. He told me that his wife had always known and had been urging him to meet you. Jacob said he was looking forward to watching you coach the team. I'm sure he never expected to meet you like that." She laughed. "I guess crashing into that church van was the best thing you've done all summer."

"Boy, I sure didn't think so at the time. You should have heard Jenny. I hope I never make her that mad again."

His mother smiled. "I'm sure you won't, Brett. What do you think you should do next?"

"Well, I don't know. I mean, I want to go back to Rome tomorrow and say, 'Hi Dad,' but how the heck do I do that?"

"I think you should do just that, Brett. But it is complicated. I've prayed about this day for a long time, and I'm so glad it's finally here. Let's pray that you and your father will now find the strength to take these next steps together."

"I've got a six-hour drive tomorrow. I guess I'll have plenty of time for praying."

"What am I thinking? You must be famished. Let me get dinner started." Brett followed her into the kitchen, asking questions he could never ask before. He wanted to know all about the young Dr. Jake.

"Oh, he was a wonderful athlete, Brett. Not as good as you, but he and our high school teams won lots of championships and awards. And he was so handsome, too. All the girls were after him."

Brett laughed. "Well, right now, Mom, he's still 6'4", but he's got a bit of a pot belly on him."

"Maybe so, Brett, but back then he was really something. His picture is in the trophy case at school."

"I never imagined."

"Of course, you didn't, dear. But now, thank God, you can."

Jamey called later that evening. "Brett, we're scheduled for a conference call with the league office at 1:00 p.m. tomorrow afternoon. They may be sending someone in later, but right now that's all we know. Can you make it?"

Brett looked over at his mother. "I'm going to have to leave early tomorrow morning, Mom," he whispered. "Got a big day." She nodded and had already started packing food for his "'long'" journey. "I'll be there," he told Jamey.

Sleep did not come easy for Brett that night. Thoughts of what might have been mingled with nervousness over confronting his father in the coming day. He thought of Jenny and tried to relax.

Brett was up early the next morning. He took a quick shower, dressed, packed his bag, and headed down-stairs. His mother was already busy in the kitchen. "Eat a good breakfast, Son. You've got a long busy day ahead of you." He had told her a little bit about the team's steroid scandal. "What do you think will happen to those three boys, Brett?"

"I don't know, Mom. Nothing good for now, I'm sure. They'll probably be suspended for the rest of this season, maybe part of next. They could be fined, but minor leaguers don't have much extra money. I know that for a fact," he said ruefully. "I think the league will figure the suspension without pay will send a strong enough message to all the other players." He hadn't told her about Vestuti's involvement or Jenny's suspicions. He would need to talk to Jenny after finding out what the league wanted to do. It was time to get the police involved and make sure he kept her safe.

Brett picked up his bag and headed for the door. Mrs. Davies handed him a huge bag of sandwiches, fruits, chips, and a small cooler filled with bottles of water. "Well, I guess this will last me till I get there, Mom," he said with a sly smile.

"Very funny, Brett." She turned serious. "When you talk to Jake, your dad, it will be fine. I know it will. He's as ready to meet his son as you are to meet your dad. God knows it's time, and He will lead both of you down the right path, as difficult as it may be."

"Well, I imagine it will be a lot tougher for him, Mom. Having to tell Nancy and the kids. And what about the church, what will they all say?"

"I know, Brett, I know. But I believe your father has been preparing for this day for a long time. He'll know what to do."

Brett gave his mother a big farewell hug and twirled her around in the air for the last time. "Gotta go, Mom. Couple things I need to take care of."

"Good luck, Brett. I love you."

"I love you, too, Mom."

16

CONFESSION

It was a quiet Thursday on the highways. Brett managed to make it through Charlotte before the morning rush hour would back things up. Soon he was crossing into South Carolina and heading toward Georgia, his mind was filled with the events of the past few days. He was determined to deal with everything, difficult as it may be, to the best of his abilities. He had decided not to talk to Jenny until after he had his meeting with Dr. Jake. Reaching for his cell phone, he hit Back Creek Church on the speed dial. The church administrator, Denise Brower, answered.

"Hi Denise. This is Brett. Is Dr. Jake in?" He was surprised how nervous he felt.

"As a matter of fact, he just got here. Hang on and I'll get him for you."

"Good morning, Jacob Fisherman." Brett now recognized the voice on the phone even more clearly.

"Hi Dr. Jake. This is Brett." *I'm talking to my dad.* He tried not to drop the phone.

"Well hello, Brett. Why are you calling me so early on this Thursday morning, young man?" He chuckled, "I thought you and the rest of the Rome Braves slept in on your days off."

Brett laughed and tried to relax. "I'm sure the rest of them are. But I'm driving back to Rome right now from Albemarle, you know, my hometown. *Of course, you know that.* I wanted to spend a little time with my mom, and this was the best chance I had."

"Is your mother OK?" Concern laced his words.

"Oh, she's fine, doing great. Listen, I need to ask a favor. I've got a meeting at the ballpark at 1 p.m. I was hoping you would have some time, say around 3 p.m. I would like to come by the church, and we could go over a few things."

"I think that would work. Let me check my calendar. Yes, we've got a Church Council meeting tonight, so I'll be here getting ready for that. What 'things' do you have on your agenda?"

Brett hesitated. *He would ask that.* "Oh, just to go over some ideas I have with the youth and the baseball program. Our season ends on Sunday. Of course, it may not. We beat the River Dogs this weekend; we'll win our division and be in the playoffs. Anyway, I didn't know if I would have a chance to talk to you before then."

"We'll all be there rooting for you and the Braves, too. But I certainly think we should get those good ideas out of your brain and onto paper before you leave. Although I do hope you'll stick around with us for a while after the season is over. Jenny still needs help with the youth, you know, even when ball season is over." The minister laughed again at his own little joke. "Something to think about, Brett."

"I guess you're right. We better add that to our agenda."

"Excellent. I'll see you at three. Have a safe trip, Brett."

Brett struggled with his emotions as he neared the Rome area. He remembered his mother's confidence that he would do the right thing. He said a quick prayer that the day would be a good one...for him and his family.

Brett arrived at the stadium and joined Jamey in the GM's office. Kiser was already on the phone. Scott, Bryce, and Wayne were sitting in chairs lined up in front of Kenny's desk. Kiser got the league official on the line. "We're all here, sir. Let me put you on the speaker."

The league office did most of the talking. Kiser took a lot of notes, and Jamey asked a few questions. The summary was quick and to the point. The players were suspended for the rest of the season and the first sixty games of next year. They would be allowed to participate in spring training. Community service and mandatory counseling sessions provided by the league were part of the "program." Before the meeting broke up, Brett spoke for the first time.

"When is this all going to be announced? Do you want us to put out a press release? There are going to be a bunch of questions once this goes public."

The league officer responded. "We'll be sending out a press release tomorrow. You will get a copy, so no need for Rome to do that as well. The news will no doubt be in all the papers by Saturday. Of course, we would have liked to have kept this under wraps until the season was over, but that's just not possible. Not a good way to end the season. You three young men need to understand your actions have not only impacted you, but those around you as well. It's a real shame."

With that, the meeting was over. Brett said a hurried good-bye and headed for the door. Jamey called out as he was leaving. "What's the big rush, Brett? Is everything OK?"

"Yeah, Jamey, no problem. I just have a few things to take care of. I'll call you tomorrow morning when I hear from Chuck."

Brett climbed into his Explorer and gunned it out of the stadium parking lot. In a few minutes, he was at Back Creek Church. He was relieved that the only other car he saw was the minister's. Dr. Jake was sitting at his desk and shuffling through some paperwork when Brett knocked on the door.

"Come on in, Brett, my boy." Spreading his large hands out over the mess in front of him, he continued. "Way too much paper and too many meetings. Sometimes I think folks believe the mission of our church is to hold meetings." He shook his head. "Enough of that, Brett. Come on and sit down. Let me hear all the great suggestions you have for our youth program."

They entered into an animated conversation as Brett talked about the new ideas he and Jenny had come up with . . . fund raising, parent involvement, community projects, youth leading a worship service. Dr. Jake peppered him with questions to get clarification and wrote down numerous notes. Brett felt like he was back in college taking an oral exam.

"These are all very good, Brett. And I can see Jenny's hand in there as well. It does appear that you two make a good team." The minister smiled at that last remark as Brett nodded, then continued. "We'll need some budget dollars for a couple of things, but maybe the fund raising will cover that. What I like is that most of this can be done totally with our youth leaders, the help of parents, and by the youth themselves. This will get them out of their comfort zone and into doing "good works" for our congregation and others in need. I like it."

"Yes sir. Thank you, sir. I know Jenny will be very glad to hear that."

"Good, anything else?" Dr. Jake peered at Brett over his eyeglasses with a quizzical smile.

Brett swallowed hard. Rubbing his sweating palms together, he remembered his mother's words . . . 'it was time'.

"Yes, sir. One other thing. Pretty big thing, actually."

"Really? Go on."

He didn't know how else to do it.

"I know you're my dad."

Dr. Jake remained silent. The big man got out of his chair and stared out the window at the empty parking lot. After a long quiet moment, he turned around to face Brett for the first time as his father. "How'd you find out, Son?"

"Someone spoke to me- - I couldn't see who- - when I was heading to the locker room from the dugout the other night. *I'm proud of you, son.* I couldn't get that voice, that phrase out of my mind." He paused before rushing ahead, the words tumbling out of his mouth. "The next morning, we left on a road trip, so I had a lot of time to think. Somehow, I don't know how or why, I remembered you congratulating me when we were with Justin after the last game. You patted me on the shoulder and said virtually the same words I heard from the stranger."

"Good detective work. So, you knew then it was me?"

Brett couldn't believe they were having this conversation. "Well sort of, I mean I thought so. But I had to make sure."

"How did you do that?"

"Pretty simple, really. It seems that Mom has a high school yearbook, and she kept the card and flowers in it that her boyfriend gave her for the prom. 'All my love', the initials JF and ED."

Dr. Jake smiled. "That was a long time ago, Brett."

"No kidding. You ought to see the flowers. Anyway, we played in Kannapolis yesterday. Since we're off today, I rented a car after the game and drove home to Albemarle. I went up into the attic to find the yearbook before Mom got home from work." Brett smiled, "You were easy to find. We even kind of look alike, but I don't think those long sideburns would work for me today."

"When your mother called me last spring and told me you were coming to Rome, I couldn't believe it. I didn't know what to do, but it seemed like a sign from God. He was telling me it's time."

"That's the same thing Mom said."

The minister looked away before replying. "She's a wonderful woman. So brave, so strong, I can hear her saying that. It was time."

They embraced as father and son for the first time. Tears came to his father's eyes. "I'm so sorry I couldn't be with you, Brett. My father was a very controlling man. Choices were made, wrong choices. I only hope you can forgive me. I'm not that young boy anymore. I don't know. I mean, I'm the pastor here, the moral leader." His father's voice filled with emotion. "And I abandoned you and your mother. How can that ever be forgiven?" The big man was trembling.

Brett took hold of his father's hands. "I know, Dad. Mom told me all about it." *I'm calling him Dad.* "I don't think right now I can say I completely understand, but I'm trying...we can catch up, can't we?"

The minister again held his son tightly. "I hope so, Brett. I think we can. We must. Come on, let's get out of here. I need some fresh air."

Brett followed him outside. They sat down on one of the benches next to the sanctuary. It was a beautiful summer day in Rome. After a few moments, Dr. Jake spoke again.

"I've been thinking about this day for a long time, Brett. What would I say? What would I do?" He shook his head. "So many years. You're right, Son. We can move ahead. I need to go home now so Nancy and I can tell our kids. That will be tough to do, but I can - - I must - - do it. Then tonight I will speak at the Council Meeting. It's past time. They need to know who you are. I need to confess and apologize. And then, well, we'll see if they still want me."

"Oh, Dr. Jake, I mean Dad, I'm sure they'll forgive you."

"You think so, Brett? We'll find out together, won't we?" He stood up and faced his son. "I want you to be there tonight, Brett. Jenny is a member of the Council, so she'll be attending. Tell you what, go get Jenny and bring her over to our house with you. I want you both there."

Brett agreed. He missed Jenny. "Good idea. This has been quite some forty-eight hours, that's for sure." He hadn't even mentioned the steroid scandal.

"OK, I've got to go back in and make a few calls. I need as many people to show up tonight as possible. I want everyone to hear me at the same time."

Brett looked at his watch as he walked to his car. It was already past five. He called Jenny on his cell.

She answered on the first ring. "Hi, Brett. I'm so glad you're home. Jamey said you went to see your mom. Is she OK?"

"Yes, she's fine. Just a good chance to see her with this day off and everything. Listen, I'd like to come to the Church Council meeting tonight. I talked to Dr. Jake this afternoon about our ideas for the youth groups and he really liked them. In fact, he's going to distribute an outline of them to everyone at the meeting. He wants us to go over to his house before we go to church to finalize the handout. Plus Dr. Jake thought it would be good for me to be with you in case there are any questions."

"Like I can't handle it?" He hoped she was teasing.

"I didn't say that. Besides, I hear it's going to be a *very interesting* Council Meeting tonight."

"'Interesting' and 'Council Meeting' do not go together around here, Brett. What's going on? Do you know something I don't?"

Wow, she has some great intuition. "Tell you what. I'll pick you up in an hour and give you the inside scoop on the way to Dr. Jake's house. Can you wait that long?"

"I guess so," she sighed. "I hope it's not anything bad. We don't need bad."

An hour later, Brett pulled into Jenny's driveway and honked the horn.

"Aren't you Mr. Romantic?" she protested as she opened the car door and slid in next to him. She gave Brett a quick kiss. "Too lazy to come to my front door and ring the bell, I guess."

He backed the car into the street and headed for the biggest meeting of young Brett Davies' life. "It's been a long season, Jenny. You need to give me a break." He pretended to be impatient with her, but it was impossible.

"Maybe I will if you tell me what the big news is. And you better do that before we get to Dr. Jake's house."

"Oh, I don't know if it's so big."

"Quit it, Brett. What's going to happen?"

"Nothing much. Till all the regular business is over. Then Dr. Jake is going to stand up and tell everyone that I, Brett Davies, am *his son.*"

Jenny screamed. "Oh my God, Brett. You're kidding, right? No, you're serious, aren't you? Are you sure? Oh, my Lord. I mean, how do you know?"

"You mean other than my mother telling me, and Dr. Jake confirming it? You mean how else do I know?"

"Brett, pull the car over. I can't breathe. I need to get out. We need to talk."

Brett turned the Explorer onto a quiet side street and cut off the engine. Jenny jumped out of the car and ran over to Brett's side. She hugged him as he got out, tears flowing.

"I don't believe it. Oh my God. Do Nancy and the kids know?"

"Nancy has always known, but they are telling the kids now." Brett quickly recapped the mysterious voice, his trip to Albemarle, the yearbook and long talk with his mother, and finally his meeting with the minister only a few hours before. "You know, I think he wanted me to find him, Jenny. It just seems that way."

"I think you're right. But it still doesn't seem right that you never knew who your father was when you were growing up. I mean, *Dr. Jake is your father*." She paused to gather her thoughts. "What happens next? What will the Council say? Will he be forced to resign?"

"I don't know. At this point, nobody does. He fathered a child out of wedlock and never told anyone other than Nancy. I guess we'll all find out together, won't we, Jen? He thinks they may ask him to resign."

"Brett, surely not. I mean we're a church. There must be forgiveness. After all, that was a long time ago."

"Careful, girl. The 'that' from a long time ago is me, and I am not that old."

She smiled and gave him another quick kiss on his cheek. "Come on, let's go. I need to have some time to talk to Nancy before the meeting. I wonder how she's handling this?"

"No telling, but when we get to church, just the two of us and Dr. Jake's family will know. So, keep your conversations quiet."

After a tearful meeting at the Fisherman's home, Brett and Jenny arrived at Back Creek Church to find the parking lot already filling with cars. "Good Lord, Brett, it looks like we're having our Easter Sunday Service." Brett didn't reply. *Looks like Dad did a good job getting everyone here.*

The regular meeting room would not hold the crowd, so the gym had been set up with chairs that were already filling to capacity. Several of the adult leaders were scrambling to bring in more chairs from adjoining rooms. Brett surveyed the noisy scene, trying to smile and make small talk with some of the parents he knew. He gazed over the throng of members, searching for a place Jenny and he could sit. A couple of Back Creek baseball players came up to him asking if Chuck Killian was really going to be in Rome tomorrow night, and could Brett introduce them.

"Sure guys. Just get there early. Chuck's going to be in a home run hitting contest at 6p.m. -- and I'm pitching."

"Wow. Sure thing, Mr. Brett. Cool." The boys sped off, eager to share their big news with other friends.

"Brett, there's Nancy over there talking to the Holloway's. Let's make sure she's holding up all right."

The minister's wife embraced them both before speaking. It had been an emotional afternoon. "Brett, thank you so much for coming over to our house and help us talk with Justin and Lisa. I want you both to know that, even though this is so hard for Jake and me, it is also very wonderful. Our God truly works in mysterious ways. Your coming to this church has been a blessing, Brett. Jake was torn by his secret about you for so many years. It was hard on him, and I know it had to be on you, too. But he's a wonderful man. I love him very much. And I'm so glad you are a part of my family." She glanced into the gym. "Well, it's about ready to start," she whispered." I guess there's no telling how the Council and the rest of the congregation will react." She looked over at Brett, "But as your father said, 'it's time'." She took out a tissue and dabbed at her eyes. "Now kids, it's preacher's wife time. How do I look?"

"Just wonderful, Mrs. Fisherman," Jenny said.

"Good. Come on, I want you two to sit with me and the kids. And please help me keep Justin quiet. He's so excited to have a '"big league"' older brother. I think he's going to burst."

The Council president, Steve Epperson, was at the microphone trying to call the meeting to order. "Please, everyone take your seat. We need to get started. Let's settle down. Thank you."

The gathering quieted and Epperson led them in an opening prayer. "We have a rather long agenda prepared. Also, as most of you know, Dr. Fisherman has asked to speak to us at the conclusion of this session. So in the interest of brevity, and to keep all of you awake," he paused to let the laughter subside, "we'll let you review the committee reports that are in your packet and dispense with the usual chairman's review. I've asked each of the committees to have a representative stay after the meeting to answer any specific questions you may have, and we'll put all that into the minutes."

Moving quickly through the agenda, the council approved the minutes from the last meeting, got a brief update from the long-range planning team, and heard special reports from the finance and stewardship committees.

"We need more money, y'all, to do what we need to do," drawled Dewey Humphrey, head of the church's capital campaign. "And I'm pretty sure it's in y'alls *pockets.*" Everyone chuckled at the all too simple truth in Humphrey's statement. Epperson again approached the microphone.

"Well, we're at the point now which I'm pretty sure is why most of you are here." He surveyed the large group in front of him. "I mean, we normally have twenty people at our Council Meetings, not two hundred." The members laughed nervously. All were anxious to find out what the minister was going to say.

"Dr. Fisherman," Epperson motioned to his pastor, "you have the floor."

Dr. Jake walked to the microphone and faced his audience. "Good evening, everyone. Please, join me in prayer." Two hundred heads bowed.

"Dear Lord, I pray tonight that You will guide my every step in the words that I speak. That my message will be clear and understood by all. And in going forward, we will always keep You first in our thoughts, prayers, and actions. In Your name we pray, Amen."

The minister looked out over his congregation. He smiled at Nancy and those sitting with her. Brett rubbed his hands together, surprised at how calm Dr. Jake seemed. The room was quiet.

"I've asked you all here tonight for a reason, a very special reason. I need to confess to you about a mistake I made, a sin actually, a long time ago. I hope and pray you'll be able to forgive me." A low murmur arose from the group as everyone struggled with what their pastor had said. The minister held up his hand for quiet. "Oh, I know. We are all sinners. We all make mistakes. Like each of you, I

certainly have made my share. But the one I must confess to you tonight is different. It happened almost thirty years ago when I was an
undergraduate student up in Chapel Hill. I was dating a wonderful
girl at the time. She was a senior in high school. We got pregnant."

A gasp arose from the congregation. Numerous eyes looked
over to Nancy who was sitting erect, looking at her husband with
pride as he continued. "Marriage was not an option and, of course,
neither was abortion. I returned to school, and she gave birth to a
blond haired, blue-eyed baby boy. Believe it or not, I used to have
blond hair." Nervous laughter came from the audience as Dr. Jake
took the microphone out of the holder. He continued speaking as
he walked over to where his family was sitting with Brett and Jenny.
"My girlfriend and I agreed to keep my identity as the father a secret. Of course, our families knew. But I was going to be a minister."
He paused and for the first time his strong voice trembled, "And I
was afraid if the church found out I had fathered a child out of wedlock, I would never be allowed to be a minister."

He stopped in front of his family. "Until today, Nancy was the
only one I had ever told about this." He looked down at his wife and
smiled. "She is so brave and so supportive. I love her very much. I am
grateful to have her as my wife." He reached down and held her hand
for a moment. "Yes, this has been my secret for all these years. But
tonight, no more secrets." He looked out at the silent audience and
continued, his voice once again strong. "I want to tell you the rest of
my story. My girl friend's name was Elizabeth Davies. She named our
son, Brett." He motioned for Brett to stand and put his arm around
his son. Together they faced the congregation. "Tonight, I am so happy to introduce you to my son . . . *Brett Davies*."

The room erupted. Applause mingled with murmurs of disap-
proval. Many of the members stood, and several came forward to
shake Brett's hand. Others remained sitting in stunned disbelief. Dr.
Jake returned to the podium and motioned for quiet. The room finally settled down. "This has been heavy on my heart for so many
years. It was time to get it out. I thank you for being here tonight,
and I pray for your forgiveness. God bless you all." He nodded to

Epperson and handed the microphone back to the Council president. The minister returned to his seat as Steve addressed the group.

"This has certainly been an unusual evening, to say the least. I guess, as with any matters involving our staff, we should turn this issue over to our Staff Parish committee. Where's Pam Mosier? Pam is your committee prepared to review Dr. Fisherman.?"

A petite red head stood and tried to speak. She was drowned out by shouts of protest.

No, we want Dr. Jake!

No review!

Let's put it to a vote!

"Quiet, please." Epperson motioned to Mosier, "Pam, what do you think?"

The congregation again settled down and waited for her response. "Well, Steve, when it comes to matters involving our Senior Pastor, the proper procedure calls for us to take this matter before our District Superintendent, Reverend Maguire." She smiled as she looked out at the concerned audience. "We will certainly recommend a decision we feel is best for Back Creek United Methodist Church."

More applause and shouts.

Tell them we want Dr. Jake.!

Yes. He is the best man for us!

Smiling, Epperson walked over and shook Dr. Jake's hand. "I'd say you've been forgiven, Doctor. We've got a congregation that knows the true meaning of forgiveness and redemption. Thank you for speaking to us tonight." He turned to face the ball player. "And Brett, let me welcome you, again, to Back Creek Church. It's nice to have you as part of our family."

Brett was still standing. "Thanks, Steve. This has been a crazy day. I thought off days for baseball teams were supposed to be easy but this one . . ."

Everyone laughed as Epperson returned to the podium. "I think it's time to get out of here. May I please have a motion to adjourn?"

It was over an hour before Brett, Jenny, and Dr. Jake's family were able to leave the church. Everyone wanted to shake Brett's hand, as well as hug the minister and his wife. Brett tried to stay close to Jenny, who smiled and kept telling everyone that it was all "amazing . . . unbelievable . . . wonderful" a few hundred times. Justin, meanwhile, was telling everyone, who already knew it, that his brother was a big league ball player.

An exhausted Jenny got into Brett's car and quickly fell asleep. As he drove her home, Brett mulled over everything that had happened in such a short time. He let a small smile come over his face. *Jacob Fisherman, my dad. What a day.* Brett had no way of knowing that tomorrow would bring another day he and Jenny would never forget.

17

BIG LEAGUE VISIT

The ringing of his cell phone jarred Brett from his restless slumber. Grabbing the annoying messenger, he checked the phone and saw that it was Jenny. It was also 7:00 a.m.

"Jenny, why in the world are you calling me so early? After last night at the church, I couldn't sleep and now . . ."

"I'm sorry, Brett, but I've got to talk to you. I'm already down at the bank. I've looked over Vestuti's personal accounts as well as the gym's. There's well over $300,000 passing back and forth in just the last three days. I found out that his assistant, you know the big guy Arnie, came in yesterday afternoon after I had left. He wanted to take $100,000 out in cash and we couldn't do it. He really gave our manager, Mr. Crampton, a hard time. Arnie refused to take a cashier's check. He demanded cash. Brett, what should I do?"

"Wow, Jenny, it sounds like they're getting ready to run. Have you talked to Detective Robinson about this?"

"I called him this morning on his cell phone." She was starting to calm down; he was starting to wake up. "I woke him up. He wasn't very happy, either. Anyway, he wants to meet with me later this morning at ten. He said to bring copies of all the bank records for the last six months but to keep it quiet. That's what I'm doing now."

"OK but be careful. I agree, keep it all quiet. Don't tell anyone except Crampton. Does he know what's going on with the steroids and everything?"

"It's too late for secrecy, Brett. Have you seen the morning paper?"

"Jenny, I just woke up, remember?"

"Well, go get it. There's a huge front-page article about the Rome Braves and the players who tested positive for steroids."

"Oh man, the league said they weren't releasing a statement till tomorrow."

"Somebody talked, Brett. They've got direct quotes from Scott Buchanan."

"I better call Jamey. He's gonna hit the roof. And Chuck and Darnell and their families are going to be here in a few hours. What a great start to the weekend."

"That's not all, Brett. In the article, Scott admits that he got the steroids from Victory Gym... *from Vestuti.*"

"Well, that explains the money, doesn't it?"

"You bet. The tellers told me that Arnie got really mad and started yelling. He said they couldn't do business in this town anymore, and that he and Vestuti would be back today to get *all* their money out."

"Listen, Jenny, you say nothing. If they come in, stay away from them."

"I'll try, Brett. I've got to go. Mr. Crampton will be here in a few minutes, and I need to get him ready for when Vestuti gets here."

"OK. Hey, don't forget we're going to Ginger's for lunch with Chuck and Darnell's families today. They can't wait to meet you – especially Sarah and Celia."

"Oh, wonderful, just what I need right now is to go to an audition."

"You'll be fine. They'll love you, because I do. I need to find out what time I need to get Chuck down to the park for the home run contest and the autographs. This is a big deal for little Rome, Georgia."

"It sure is. Are you sure you really know him? I mean..."

"Yes, Jenny, I know Chuck very well, and Sarah and the kids."

"OK, I believe you. I'll be there and so will most of the Back Creek Church baseball teams as well. Plus Dr. Jake, I mean your father, and his family. Last night seems like a long time ago. Did it really happen?"

"You ought to see it from my side, Jenny. You stay cool. I'll see you in a few hours. I'll pick you up at the bank at 9:45."

"That should work. We're meeting the detective at ten. I love you, Brett. Thanks for listening to me."

Brett hung up the phone and headed for the shower. His mind was spinning. *Got to get a paper and call Jamey.* His phone was ringing again before he could dry off. It was Jamey.

"Brett, can you get down to the stadium right away?"

"I already heard, Jamey. I can be there in ten minutes." Brett threw his clothes on and raced out to his car. Speeding through the quiet Rome streets, he stopped to buy a paper and a cup of coffee. He pulled into the stadium parking lot and headed for Kenny's office. Jamey and Kiser were waiting, along with another man who Brett did not recognize. The room was tense. His mind flashed back to a similar scene in Principal Harland's office the previous fall. The GM spoke first.

"Brett, when I called Jamey Tuesday night and told you about our three players who tested positive, I thought I had made it clear for everyone to stay quiet and let the league office do the talking. But now," he picked up the newspaper that was lying on his desk, "obviously all that has changed."

"I know, Kenny, I just heard about all this myself. What was Scott thinking? Has anyone talked to him?"

"We'll find out soon enough," Jamey answered. "Scott will be here in five minutes. Brett, this is Phil Wilhite, with the league office. He came up this morning from Atlanta when all this hit the fan."

"Nice to meet you finally, Brett," Wilhite shook Brett's hand. His firm grip and muscular build were that of a former athlete who was still in pretty good shape. "But maybe not quite like this. I've been following your story. I remember watching you pitch in Atlanta a few years back at the end of the season. Coming back from that shoulder injury – you've been through a lot, haven't you?"

"Yes, sir, I think you could say that." *And he doesn't even know about the information Jenny has.*

There was a light knock on the door. A very nervous Scott Buchanan walked into the room. Brett looked his young pitching star in the eye. "Sit down, Scott. We need to know what happened. You weren't supposed to talk with anyone, and now this." Brett pointed to the paper on Kiser's desk. "The Rome Braves and steroids are all over the front page. You're the only source quoted. What were you thinking?"

"I'm sorry, Coach, Skip, Mr. Kiser. I didn't mean to. I was tricked, honest."

"Tell us what happened, Scott." Jamey was trying to remain calm.

"Yes, sir. You see, after we got back Wednesday night a bunch of us went to the Waffle House, just like we do a lot of times after games. Bryce and Wayne weren't with us. I was the only one who – well, you know. But I didn't say anything to our guys."

"Go on."

"We're in there eating and just talking and stuff. In walks Clay Pruitt from the paper. He's seen us down there several times, so he knows that's where we sometimes hang out. Anyway, he sits down and asks if he can talk to me privately. I agree. I guess that wasn't the smartest thing to do."

The three men said nothing as Scott plunged ahead with his story.

"We sit down off to the side, and he goes through a little small talk about the season and everything. Then out of the blue, he tells me he knows all about the three of us flunking the drug test. He says they plan to run a big front-page story on us in the Friday paper. He asks me if I want to make a statement, but I told him no, I wasn't going to comment on anything. Clay says OK and gets up to leave. But before he does, he turns around and asks me, 'I guess you guys got what you needed from Victory Gym, right?' I must have mumbled something like, 'I guess so' or whatever. He just smiled and said, 'I thought so' and walked out the door. After he left, I sat there and realized what I'd done. I felt so stupid. I'm sorry. I was tired. It was late. I just didn't think."

Wilhite spoke next. "Scott, I'm Phil Wilhite with the league office. I handle all our legal issues." He glanced over at the other men in the room. "I imagine you and I will be spending some time together, along with Bryce and Wayne, of course."

"Yes, sir."

Wilhite addressed the whole group. "We have been suspicious of Victory Gym and its owner, Vestuti, for several months now. We had hoped to keep our investigation private as we gathered more information."

"You better hurry, Phil." All eyes turned toward Brett. "Victory Gym banks where my girlfriend works here in town. She's the manager over all the cashiers. She's noticed unusually large sums of money coming through their account recently. I'm talking several hundred thousand dollars. Yesterday, one of Vestuti' s assistants came into the bank and wanted to pull $100,000 out... in cash. The bank couldn't do it, and he refused to take a bank check. He got real mad and real loud. He said he and Vestuti would be back today to get their money, and the bank better have it ready. I think they're leaving town as fast as they can pack their cash and their bags. I bet that Clay guy talked to them yesterday, too. That must be what got them all worked up along with the article in the paper this morning."

"So, she knows all about their banking transactions?" Wilhite asked.

"Yep, everything. In fact, she's making copies of the last six months' records right now. I'm going with her for a meeting later this morning with a detective who's been investigating Vestuti."

"That would be Detective Robinson. We've been working with him all along on this," Wilhite advised the group. "Those bank records are going to be very helpful, Brett. But tell your girlfriend to be careful. I've checked the history on these guys, and they have a nasty background."

Kiser sighed and stood up behind his desk. "This is crazy. Our team is tied for first with only three games. We've got the biggest weekend of the year planned, not to mention that Chuck Killian will be here tonight to meet all our fans. And we're dealing with all *this crap*." He paused to regain his composure. "Wayne and Bryce will be here soon. Scott, I want the three of you to sit down with Mr. Wilhite. You can use our conference room. Tell him everything you know about this whole mess. I'd like to see Vestuti, and his stooges put away for a long time. And you need to put all this behind you too, Scott. I can't guarantee anything, but I'm pretty confident that if you do everything right from here on out, the Braves will have a spot for you in the organization next year. Wayne and Bryce, too. But it's all up to you boys."

Brett put his hand on his young pitching star's shoulder. "You can do that, can't you, Scott? Promise me that you will."

"I promise. Don't worry. I know I screwed up big time. It's all on me, and I can fix it. You'll see."

Brett looked at his watch and saw that it was 9:30. Jenny's meeting with Robinson was in thirty minutes and he needed to be there. "Kenny, Chuck and his family are driving up from Atlanta this morning. Jenny and I are meeting them for lunch along with a high school friend of mine and his family. I just need to know what time you need Chuck and me back here this afternoon."

"Plan to have him on the field no later than 6 p.m., Brett. We're opening up the gates at 5:30. We've told everyone that Chuck's home run hitting contest will start around 6:15. The Braves are donating a thousand dollars for each home run he hits to our United Way, so it's a big deal."

"Ok, we'll be ready."

"One more thing, Brett. Can you pitch to Chuck in the home run contest? I think everyone would get a big kick out of that."

Brett smiled. "Sure, no problem. In fact, we were already planning to do just that. Chuck's hit plenty of homers off me in practice games. A few more for charity won't hurt at all."

Brett called Jenny as he walked to his car. "Please hurry, Brett. I'm all by myself. Mr. Crampton stayed at the bank in case Vestuti shows up. We even had extra cash brought in so we could pay him everything if they demand it. *It's over $250,000, Brett.*"

"I'm on the way. Are we meeting at the detective's office?"

"Yes, he's in the Government Building, third floor, room 302. They'll be expecting us."

A few minutes later they arrived at their destination. Detective Donald Robinson stood to greet the young couple as they entered his office. He was a tall, slender man, probably in his late forties based on the touches of gray in his receding hair line. Brett noticed his eyes, piercing and focused, as the detective looked his guests over through wire-rimmed glasses.

After brief introductions and baseball talk, Robinson asked Jenny to show him the bank records. He looked over the documents and kept a steady stream of questions flowing as he scribbled furiously in his notebook. *Who made the deposits? Did she recognize any names on the checks Vestuti had written? When did she first notice the cash activity increasing?* Brett sat there and took it all in. Jenny was poised and calm, working hard to remember all the details for the detective.

The review went on for almost an hour as they poured over the bank records of Victory Gym. Glancing at his watch, Robinson addressed Brett and Jenny. "I've got to leave in a few minutes." He smiled at Brett. "Seems like I've got a meeting over at the Braves' stadium. Your friend, Mr. Wilhite, wants me there when he talks to our three young men."

"Mr. Robinson, I know my guys are guilty of being stupid. But I certainly hope they're not going to jail or anything."

The detective laughed before answering. "Oh, not them, Brett. Not them." He looked over to Jenny. "Do you really think Vestuti and his people made all this money selling steroids? That's just the tip of the iceberg, young lady."

Jenny reached for Brett's hand. "What do you mean? What else is going on?"

"Quite a bit. It seems that our friends at Victory Gym have had a nice little drug store operating out of their back room for quite some

time. If they didn't have it, they found it, brought it in, and sold it —
for a tidy profit, I'm sure. HGH and other steroids are just a small part
of this. We are reasonably certain that they've been dealing cocaine,
heroin, marijuana, meth, and all the other cocktails. Thanks to you,
Jenny, we can put the final pieces together and close in."

"Sounds good and I hope you do," Brett responded. "But like I
told Mr. Wilhite, you better move fast. They're trying to get all their
money out of the bank, and then they'll all be off to who knows
where."

"I'm aware of all that," Robinson assured the young couple.
"We'll track Vestuti and the rest of them down no matter where
they go."

Brett and Jenny walked out of the building with the detective.
Robinson turned to head for his car and offered a final warning. "Be
very careful, you two. The newspaper article has blown this wide
open. Vestuti's going to be scared, and we know from his past that
he's very dangerous when cornered. Jenny, if they come into your
bank and want all their money, just give it to them and watch them
leave. Let us do the dirty work."

"Yes, sir," Jenny assured him. Her voice was trembling for the
first time. "I'll be careful."

Jenny and Brett went over to Brett's car. As they were beginning
to discuss what to do next, his cell phone rang. It was Chuck.

"Hey, old man, how you doing? We just checked in to the Rome
Hilton and we're living in the lap of luxury, my friend. They gave
us the Executive Suite; can you imagine that? Good thing, too, because Darnell and his family just got here. They're on the other side
of us. At least the kids have some walls to bounce off of."

Brett smiled as he listened to his friend, then whispered to
Jenny, "And he's got no idea of all the stuff going on with us right
now . . . That's great, Chuck. Glad to hear they're taking good care of
you and Darnell. Listen, it's getting close to noon. Let's have lunch
over at Ginger's. It's a great place and not too far from where you
are. Great barbecue, chicken, home-cooked veggies, good southern cooking . . . plus, they know who I am."

"I'm sure they do," Chuck interrupted, "after all, you are the star pitcher and pitching coach of the Rome Braves."

"And you're talking to him," Brett said. "You need to show a little respect. We're only about fifteen minutes from Ginger's. Everything's close in this town."

"You got that right – not like Atlanta traffic, that's for sure. I'll GPS it, and we'll meet you over there. I'm sure Darnell is ready to go. That boy is always hungry."

"Great. We've got a lot to catch you up on. I can't wait for everyone to meet Jenny," he said as he winked at his now blushing companion.

"I've got a feeling Sarah will like her. That's good enough for me. By the way, your team 'story' managed to dominate the Atlanta sports pages this morning. What a mess. I guess these kids will never learn, will they?"

"I think these three will, and I hope they are scared to death. Heck, I hope our whole team has learned a lesson. Like I said, Chuck, there's a lot going on. You don't even know the half of it yet."

Brett drove to the bank. Jenny got out of his car and ran inside to see if Vestuti had been there. In a few moments she was back outside and jumped in alongside Brett for the ride to Ginger's. "Vestuti called Mr. Crampton, Brett. He told Brian that he would be at the bank at 5 p.m., right before we close. Vestuti told him he wants all of his money, and he wants it in cash."

"OK, you know what Robinson said to do, so just do it."

"I know, and I told that to Mr. Crampton. Still, it's scary. You know what I mean? Those people are just so *icky*."

"You're right, babe. But 'icky' may be too nice a term at this point."

They arrived at the restaurant, and a few moments later Chuck drove up with Darnell and their families packed into his big Ford Excursion. Introductions were made. Brett was amazed at how at ease Jenny seemed. *If the Vestuti thing wasn't enough, now she's meeting my two best friends and their wives.* Their group was ushered to two large tables that had been set up after Brett had called to tell the restaurant they were coming. The kids were seated together, and the adults settled in next to them.

"So, Jenny, I think we'd all like to hear your version as to how you two met." Sarah smiled warmly. They all waited for Jenny's side of the tale Brett had told them.

Jenny laughed. "Well, let's just say we bumped into each other."

"And the rest is history?" Celia Motley offered.

"More like hysteria, actually," she answered, reaching for Brett's hand. "Isn't that right, my little snookie wookie?"

Chuck and Darnell couldn't stop laughing at their friend. "Look at that, Darnell. They're holding hands. Isn't that cute?"

Sarah shook a disapproving finger at her husband. Brett was finally able to get a few words in. "Let's just say that I've learned not to contradict this young lady. I bet you didn't know that she's even turned me into a God-fearing, Bible-thumping, Sunday School teacher for a bunch of wild teenagers."

"So, she worked miracles with you, old man?"

"That is very correct, Mr. Big League Star. And she can hold my hand as long as she wants."

"Maybe that will be for a long time, right Jenny?" Sarah asked.

Jenny blushed but recovered as she turned her attention to Brett and Chuck. "Do you two always talk like that to each other?'

"You don't even want to know, Miss Jenny," Darnell interjected. "All I can say is it's a good thing they like each other. I'd sure hate to hear what they said if they didn't."

"So, how did you get to know Brett and Chuck, Darnell? Did you play baseball with them, too?"

Celia was laughing now. "Look at my husband, Jenny. Do you think that big old man was built to play baseball?"

"I'm not that old," Darnell pouted.

The laughter continued as the waitress arrived with cold pitchers of sweet tea and warm baskets of hush puppies for the tables. She took their lunch order – barbecue for the adults, hot dogs and burgers for the kids – and the chatter resumed with the men and women now engaged in separate conversations.

"What exactly is going on with this steroid stuff, Brett?" Chuck asked. "Is it just those three or are there more?"

"As far as I know, it's just the three." He looked over at Darnell. "I swear when I found out, I felt just like I was back in Principal Harland's office last fall."

"Don't remind me."

"I know, Darnell, but it was the same crap. Wanting to get faster, stronger, and doing it all for the team. This time they were told there was a masking agent in the doses that would keep them looking clean."

"That didn't work, did it?"

"Nope, Chuck, it sure didn't. Anyway, the quick version of 'the rest of the story' is that we've confirmed that they were getting the drugs right here in Rome at a place called Victory Gym. They've been running thousands of dollars through the bank here in town where Jenny works. She was thinking something fishy was going on, and she was right. In fact, before we came here, we had a meeting with a local detective who has been following these people. Turns out they're dealing a lot more than just steroids."

Darnell snorted. "Sounds like a great group of guys you have here in Rome. I'd like to get my hands on them."

"Yeah, a great group. You know, Jenny told me they were icky the first time I met the owner and his partner. I met them right here in Ginger's."

"Icky?"

"Yep, 'icky.' Doesn't get any worse than that for my Jenny."

The waitress arrived with their orders. The men stopped talking to concentrate on the heaping plates of hot food in front of them. The ladies did the same yet managed to keep their conversation going. Brett did not pay much attention until he overheard Jenny use the words 'Dad' and 'Brett' in the same sentence. He looked over at Sarah, whose mouth had dropped wide open. "You don't mean it, Jenny. Brett, is this true?"

"Yes, Sarah, it surely is."

"What are you three talking about?" Chuck grumbled as he continued to shovel in more barbecue and slaw.

"Nothing much, guys. Just that I found my dad."

"*What?!*"

"You heard me. Turns out he's the minister at Jenny's church. I coached his son, or should I say my brother, on our baseball team this summer."

"But how did you find out?" Chuck and Darnell were now staring at their friend.

"It's a long story."

"We've got time," four voices responded in unison.

Brett did most of the talking for the rest of the meal with Jenny throwing in a few words like "blessing," "amazing," and "wonderful." He related the events – from the mysterious stranger to the trunk in Albemarle, and finally the meeting at Back Creek Church the previous evening. The conversations continued as they left the restaurant and were at their cars. "So, am I going to meet this guy, your dad, tonight?" Chuck asked.

"You bet. In fact, there's going to be a big crowd of Back Creek Church members there at the game, including Dr. Jake. Right, Jenny? Seems like there's a story going around that a big league Braves star is in town to put on a hitting show and sign autographs. We expect a sellout."

"Braves hitting star. Is that you, Chuck?" Darnell asked politely. They all broke up in laughter one more time and said their good-byes. Jenny hugged Sarah, Celia, and all the kids. Sophie assured Jenny she could be her friend. The group promised to see each other later that evening. As the crowd was piling back into Chuck's Excursion, Sarah motioned Brett over to her.

"She's wonderful, Brett. I know your mom will just love her. We all do."

"Thanks, Sarah. This has truly been an amazing summer. I've been very lucky."

Brett drove Jenny back to the bank. She gave him a particularly big kiss before she got out of the car. "So, did I pass the audition, Mr. Davies?"

"Yes, I believe so, Miss Lynnville," Brett replied. "You did very well today. Of course, you still have to meet my mother. I trust you'll do equally well there, too."

"Well, I know your father likes me, so I think I've got a good chance. Besides, you still need to meet my parents and my brothers."

"Very funny. Please don't remind me. Now remember you need to get everyone down to the park early tonight. They are opening the gates at 5:30, and we're taking batting practice from 5:30 to 6:00. Chuck hits last. That's when I'm pitching to him, and with every home run he hits, the Braves will donate a thousand dollars to our United Way. Then he'll be signing autographs alongside our dugout until the game starts."

"No problem," Jenny assured him. "I just need to get Vestuti out of the bank as quickly as possible, and we'll be there. Imagine all this. We've got a big league hitting star, Chuck Killian, in our very own little town of Rome. Just amazing."

"Don't get so excited. Besides, I knew him when he was just a scared rookie in the minors, just like I was. Sarah's the reason for his success. That much I'm sure of."

"Ah yes, a good man definitely needs a good woman."

"So, I've heard. I sure hope I find one some day."

"Very funny," she sniffed as she got out of the car.

"Hey, remember," he called out as she headed to the bank, "don't do anything stupid, OK?"

She waved but didn't look back. "I won't."

⸺⬥⸺

Later that afternoon, Brett picked Chuck up at the hotel, and they headed for the ballpark. Darnell was in charge of getting the rest of the troops together and bringing them down in Chuck's big truck in time for the start of the "Brett and Chuck" show. It was a beautiful warm summer evening for baseball, and there was already a big crowd entering the stadium when Brett pulled into the players' parking area. Walking to the clubhouse entrance, they were recognized by the fans, and several rushed over to get a closer look at their heroes. Fortunately, extra security in the form of the Rome police department was already on the scene. They were able to usher the two stars into the Braves' locker room. Jamey came over to greet them.

"Great to see you again, Chuck. You guys have really been tearing the Eastern Division up this season."

"Yeah, nineteen games ahead with only twenty-five to play. I'd say we're in pretty good shape. I'm just glad they could give me the day off so I could get up here tonight. I really wanted to keep my commitment to you guys after the rain cancelled everything last month. And this is the last weekend we had, right?"

"Yep, this is it for us. You want to get dressed in my office?"

"Nah, just find me a locker out there with all the guys. I brought my gear, including," he winked at Brett, "a couple of my favorite bats."

"Skip, should I just lay them right in there for our hero tonight?" Brett asked playfully. "I mean, if I give him the real deal, the Grade A Davies' stuff, this big crowd will probably go home disappointed."

"That's right, Brett." Jamey replied. "Can't cheat the paying customers, can we?"

The Rome players had been eyeing Chuck since he and Brett walked in. A few had met him in spring training, but for most this was their first time near a real big league star. Brett called the room to attention.

"Friends and Roman baseball players, lend me your ears. Let me introduce a great friend of mine. Someone who was on my first minor league team and, through my careful guidance over the years . . ." Everyone laughed as Chuck rolled his eyes. "Stay with me, guys," Brett urged. "Ahem, as I was saying, through my careful guidance over the years, he has grown to where he is now – an All-Star player and MVP candidate with the Atlanta Braves. *Let's give it up for Chuck Killian.*" The young players clapped and rushed forward to introduce themselves to the Braves star. Chuck was clearly enjoying himself, making a special effort to speak to each player.

The crowd roared as Chuck appeared in his Atlanta uniform with the familiar number 26 on the back. Brett followed him onto the diamond and turned to check the stands. The Back Creek Church group was sitting in their familiar place. He waved to all of them. He grabbed Chuck and pointed up to the stands. "There, do you see the tall guy with glasses and a gray beard wearing the Braves cap? That's Dr. Jake. That's my dad."

"Everyone's wearing a Braves cap," Chuck muttered as he surveyed the packed stands.

Dr. Jake waved and pointed at the two players. "OK, now I see him." Chuck waved back. "Wow, your dad right here in Rome. Just amazing. Is Jenny up there yet?"

Brett searched the stands but didn't see her. He walked to the edge of the railing and called out to Dr. Jake, who was about fifteen rows up. *"Where's Jenny?"*

"I tried to call her a few minutes ago," he hollered back, "but she didn't answer. I'll keep trying."

Brett looked at Chuck and shrugged. "It's still early. She'll be here soon. Come on, the show's getting ready to start."

The Braves players finished hitting. The batting cage was rolled away as Chuck approached the plate. The team's radio announcer, Lane Michael, was acting as emcee for the event and introduced Chuck to the crowd. The roar was deafening. Brett stepped up onto the mound as Chuck waved, tipped his hat, and held his bat in the air for all his fans. Brett glanced back into the stands, but still didn't see Jenny. Darnell and the kids were in their seats. Sarah and Celia had somehow found the Back Creek group and were now sitting in the aisle talking excitedly with Dr. Jake and Nancy.

How'd they find them? And what on earth are they saying about me? This can't be good.

Penny jumped in behind the plate to catch for Brett. Players for both teams were out of the dugout and gathered near the home plate area. Cameras and cell phones clicked as Michael announced the rules of the contest. Chuck would take five practice swings, and then the home run hitting contest would begin. The rules were the same as the contest held during the Major League Baseball All-Star competition. Any swing not resulting in a home run over the fence would be an out. Ten outs and the contest would be over. And, of course, the big news. With every home run Chuck hits, the Braves would donate one thousand dollars to the Rome United Way. There were even special gold "Money Balls" that would be used exclusively after the ninth out. Five thousand dollars would be the donation for each gold ball Chuck delivered over the fence.

Brett fired his first pitch over the middle of the plate. Chuck swung effortlessly and deposited the ball far beyond the left field fence. The crowd roared its approval. There was similar success on the next pitches. Chuck had hit three home runs with his five practice swings. Time now for the real thing.

The outfield was covered with members of the Rome Little League, including Justin Fisherman and other Back Creek Church players. All were in their team uniforms. Brett smiled as he surveyed the scene. *They are going to have a blast.* The boys and girls were anxious to see lots of balls sail over their heads into the parking lot beyond. But they were also hoping to catch a long fly ball off the bat of Chuck Killian. Everyone was fired up and on edge. Brett took another quick look into the stands. Jenny's seat was still empty.

Chuck was being more deliberate now, taking Brett's first three pitches. Brett knew the slugger liked the inside pitch a little below the waist so he could turn on it and drive the ball over the fence. His next pitch hit the spot, and the results were instant. Chuck blasted a long fly ball over the left field fence. A thousand dollars to the United Way.

Brett continued to throw smoothly, and Chuck responded. The capacity crowd cheered with every long home run, and they moaned when the occasional fly ball fell short. Chuck reached nine outs with fifteen home runs. A fantastic effort worth $15,000 for the Rome charity.

The Braves' bat boy replaced Brett's bucket with the gold Money Balls for Chuck's final swings of the night. Brett looked in at his friend. Chuck smiled and waved that he was fine, although sweat was dripping off him from his efforts. The fans were on their feet. Just one more out left and $5,000 for each homer. Brett paused to wipe the moisture off his forehead from the warm evening. "You ready, Chuck?"

"Bring 'em on, old man. I got a few swings left in me."

Brett's first two pitches with the gold ball were off the mark but not the third. Chuck swung mightily and drove the ball deep over the left field fence and into the parking lot. *Someone is going to find a special souvenir tonight.* The crowd continued their applause as Brett delivered another pitch. *SMACK.* Another long drive by the Braves' hitting star lofted over the fence.

Everyone was on their feet. Lane Michael announced excitedly that the Braves' donation was now at $25,000 and the noise level increased. Brett looked up into the stands. Chuck's and Darnell's families had moved over to the Back Creek section and were now standing next to Dr. Jake and Nancy. Brett pointed to his fans, waved, and reached into the bag for another gold ball. His pitch was a little off from the "perfect" spot, but Chuck swung and knocked a hard line drive into the outfield that scattered the majority of Rome little leaguers. The contest was over.

Chuck walked toward the mound to embrace his friend. Together they waved one more time to the fans and headed for the Rome dugout so Chuck could cool off before the autograph session started. Brett looked up into the stands again. He still did not see Jenny. The empty seat next to Dr. Jake and Nancy was noticeable. *Where is she?*

18

RESCUE

B rett got to the dugout and took his cell phone out of his equipment bag. There were no missed calls from Jenny. He dialed her number. It went immediately to voice mail. "Hey, babe, where the heck are you?" He tried to not sound worried. "Your seat's waiting for you up there with all the Back Creek folks. Game starts in twenty minutes. Hope you get here quick. Bye. Love ya.'"

Chuck was getting ready to head over to the autograph area. "What's the matter, Brett? You're looking pretty worried in spite of that fantastic pitching performance."

"Ah nothing, I hope, Chuck. It's just that Jenny's not here. The bank closed over an hour ago. She didn't want to miss our home run contest. I don't know . . ."

"Stuck in Rome's Friday evening traffic, no doubt. She'll be here soon enough."

Brett tried to turn his attention to the upcoming game, the first of an important three-game series that would determine the division champion. Grabbing a dry jersey out of his bag, he toweled the sweat off, changed shirts, and headed for the bullpen. Chuck was already engulfed by young and old fans who pleaded for autographs on baseballs, hats, t-shirts, and anything else they could find. Two Rome police officers and three Braves ushers were fighting a losing battle to keep the line organized. There was no doubt about the popularity of the Atlanta Braves' young hitting star with the Rome fans.

Barry Morris, tonight's starting pitcher, had already begun throwing in the bullpen when Brett arrived. "How you feel, Barry?"

"Good, Coach. This big crowd and having Chuck here, it's a real rush for all of us. We really want to play well this weekend, finish the season strong. After all that bad news about Scott, Wayne, and Bryce, we just want to show everyone we're better than that." He stopped throwing to wipe his face with a towel. "You know, I thought I knew Scott pretty well, but I had no idea he was doing steroids. I mean, he told me he felt like he was wearing down, and he didn't think his ball had the usual pop."

"That's what he told me, too," Brett replied. "Pretty poor excuse for doing something stupid."

"He feels awful. I hope the Braves give him a second chance. He's got great stuff. He's better than me, that's for sure. I need my A+ game tonight."

"I understand, but don't get too hyper, Barry. Stay within yourself and throw strikes. After your first pitch, it'll just be another game." Brett winked at his hurler as he headed back to the Braves dugout. "But one we need to win."

The Braves jumped out early on the River Dogs in the bottom of the first, getting a three-run homer from Jimmy Bavista, who was starting in Bryce's place in the outfield. Morris was on his game, moving the ball in and out, keeping the Charleston batters guessing. The score remained 3-0 going into the ninth, when the River Dogs got the first two batters on base against the tiring Braves hurler. In the dugout, Jamey looked over at Brett and nodded his head. Calling time, Brett strode to the mound to check on Morris. Penny met them there.

"What do you think, Jerry? How's his stuff? Can he finish?"

The catcher shot a quick look at Barry before responding. "He's starting to leave the ball up over the plate a little, Coach. He's pitching a heck of a game, though."

"I know — so let's not ruin it." Brett turned to Morris, "Great game, Barry. You showed this crowd what our team is made of." He took the ball from his pitcher's hand and patted him on the shoulder. "We'll bring Maury in to finish this thing up."

Brines, the Braves' ace closer, hustled in from the bullpen. Brett handed him the baseball. "We need three outs, Maury. Just like you've done for us all season." The crowd was on their feet, cheering for Morris as he walked to the dugout. Brett followed him. Looking up in the stands, there was still no Jenny. Dr. Jake caught his eye and motioned for Brett to meet him alongside the dugout.

"What's going on, Dad? Is it about Jenny?"

"I called Brian Crampton at home, Brett. He would have been at the bank with Jenny at the end of the day. He did see Jenny leave."

"Yeah, but where . . ."

"Apparently Vestuti and one of his goons – Arnie, I think – got there just before the bank closed and demanded their money. Jenny took care of getting the funds together while Brian tried to keep them quiet in his office. He said they were like mad men. The security officer was still there, so he helped Brian escort Vestuti and the other guy out of the bank to their car. Jenny had the money. Brian said he saw her hand it over to Vestuti. He and Arnie got in their car and drove off."

Brett looked over his shoulder. Brines had finished his warm-up pitches and was talking to Penny on the mound. The game was about to resume. "Then what happened?"

"That's it. Jenny and Brian went back into the bank and finished closing up. They left the building together. He offered to walk Jenny to her car, but she said she was fine and needed to get to the ballpark."

"So, what time was that?"

"He wasn't sure. He thought it was close to six."

"OK, I've got to get back to the game. I'll talk with you after it's over."

The minister grabbed Brett's arm. "I hope she's all right, Son. My instincts tell me something is terribly wrong."

"I agree."

Brett got back in the dugout. Jamey shot him a puzzled look. Chuck walked over.

"What's up, old man?"

"Jenny's missing. She left the bank for the ballpark right after giving Vestuti his money. That was at six. She's not here, and no one's seen her. She's not answering her phone, either."

"What do you think?"

Brett's face was grim as he looked over at his friend. "Chuck, I think after the game, you, Darnell, and I need to drive out to Victory Gym and *ask them*."

"OK, my man. That's just what we'll do."

To Brett's relief, Brines was at the top of his game. He induced the first batter to hit an easy ground ball that Cabaniski and Jackson turned into a nifty double play. That was followed a few pitches later by a called strike three. Braves win, 3-0.

Chuck and Brett hustled back to the locker room and changed out of their uniforms. "Whew, no shower tonight, Chuck. I don't think anyone will want to be in a car with us except Darnell." Outside in the parking lot they met a worried Dr. Jake, who was surrounded by his Back Creek members. Sarah, Celia, Darnell, and their kids were also there. It was obvious from the looks on all their faces that the minister had given them the same report.

"Dad, I think Vestuti has something to do with this. I'm going to head over to Victory Gym with Darnell and Chuck. We'll take Chuck's car because nobody knows it. Here are my car keys. If you can get Sarah and Celia and the kids back to the hotel, that would be great. We shouldn't be gone too long."

"Darnell, you be careful." His wife hugged her big man. "Take care of those two. And for God's sake, *find Jenny*."

Dr. Jake gathered the group around him. They held hands as he said a prayer for safety and guidance, and their Jenny. The three friends climbed into Chuck's Excursion and drove out of the parking lot.

It only took a few minutes to reach their destination. The gym was closed. There were no lights on. A full moon illuminated the building.

"Pull around to the side, Chuck," Brett whispered. "Let's get a closer look." Brett dialed Jenny's cell phone again as Chuck edged his car along the building. Still no answer. Chuck parked his car, and the three men got out. Brett motioned for Darnell to head toward the back of the building. Brett wanted to explore the front more carefully. Chuck would keep watch in both directions. Walking along the side of the structure, Brett peeked around to the front entrance but still saw no activity. Looking back at Chuck, he saw Darnell in the moonlight, waving for Brett to rejoin them. He ran to his friends.

"What's up, Darnell? Did you see something?"

"Darn right, I did. One car and a large van. I saw couple of guys carrying boxes that looked like files and putting them in the van. You can see them pretty good with the light inside the building back there. I think the door they're coming out of is near a loading dock or something. I didn't try to get any closer. Came right back here."

"Sounds like we caught them while they're still packing to leave." Brett thought for a moment. "How dark is it in the alley, Darnell?'

"Dark enough. They won't see my black skin, that's for sure."

Brett glanced over at Chuck and grinned. "That's why we brought you along, Darnell. Let's go take another look." The three of them walked to the back of the building and peered around the edge. The area was quiet again. No one going in or out.

"Listen, guys, I've been in this building before. I worked out here once, and Vestuti gave me the grand tour. It's an old, converted grocery store. There's a long storage area all along the back. The receiving dock is in the middle, and a little supervisor office just inside. I think there are two exit doors, one door is next to the dock, and the other one comes out of the office." He took another long look down the alley. "I can see some light from where I think the office is. I'm going down for a closer look. The car and van are on the other side of the dock. I don't think anyone will see me."

Pressing close to the brick siding, Brett crouched down and inched his way toward the light. It was about ninety feet away.

Home to first. He finally got to a point beneath the window and rose up to peer over the ledge into the little room. As his eyes adjusted to the light, he saw a desk and several chairs. The door opened and Vestuti walked in, followed by Arnie. As Brett watched, Arnie went back into the storage area, returning a few moments later, pushing a young woman into the room. *It was Jenny.* Brett's heart raced. *What do I do now?*

Her hands were tied behind her. She looked tired and her hair was a mess. She was also mad. He heard her speak. "You'll never get away with this, Vestuti. You'll get caught. I swear, you and Arnie will be going to jail for a long time."

Vestuti snapped back. "Shut up. You've already talked too much to your detective buddy and your boyfriend. I couldn't take any chances that you'd screw things up for me before we got out of town. Tie her up, Arnie." Vestuti looked at his watch as Arnie wrestled Jenny into the chair and bound her arms and legs to it. "We'll be out of here in less than an hour. Then maybe I'll let your lover boy know where you are." He laughed derisively. He was unaware that "lover boy" was less than ten feet away. "We'll be long gone before they find you." He leaned forward into her sweat-streaked face. "Remember what I said," he hissed. "No cops – or I'll make sure no one ever finds you."

Brett turned around to race back to his waiting friends and tried to think of a plan of attack. They couldn't call anyone. No, they had to do this on their own. "She's in there," he gasped. "They've got her tied up, but she's OK. Somehow, they found out we went to the police, so Vestuti grabbed her to make sure she didn't talk to anyone while they packed up. They plan to leave Rome tonight." He shook his head. "What have I done? I never should have let it get this far."

"Be quiet, old man." Chuck clasped his hand on Brett's shoulder. "It's not your fault. What we have to do now is get her out of there."

"I know. You're right. Let me think." Brett racked his brain, searching for an answer. "OK, listen. We've got to create a diversion. As far as I can tell, it's just the two of them, Vestuti and Arnie."

"That's right," Darnell interjected. "I didn't see anyone else."

"Good. What I'll do is go around to the entrance and start banging on the door. I'll be calling out for Vestuti. Really create a ruckus. That'll get him to come to the front, maybe both of them. The dock door is open. When you hear me yelling, you two should be able to slip into the building. Jenny will be in the little office on the other side of the dock doors. The only question is where Arnie is going to be. Once you get inside, stay hidden until you locate him." Brett paused, thinking his plan through. "I need to make Vestuti open the door so I can get in. That'll be the only way I agree to shut up. Once I get inside, I'll get Vestuti into a big argument about Jenny and steroids and everything. That should be easy to do. All the screaming should bring Arnie up to the front, too. When I see him, I'll start arguing with him, yelling his name. That way you know I got both of them up there. That should give you the opening you need. Any questions?"

Chuck spoke up first. "Nah, sounds like a pretty good plan. Divide and conquer. You could have a nice career with the FBI, Brett, if this baseball thing doesn't pan out."

"Thanks for the advice, Chuck," Brett answered. "Listen, one more thing. Once you've got Jenny safe, call Detective Robinson." Brett gave the number to Chuck, who quickly punched it into his cell phone. "Maybe we can get the cops here while I'm still arguing with these two crooks. If they try to run out the back, you guys can have some fun with them."

Darnell chuckled and rubbed his meaty hands together. "I need me some fun tonight." Brett and Chuck smiled. The thought of Darnell wailing away on the two drug dealers was indeed a nice one.

Brett was ready. "All right, let's do it."

Darnell looked up into the moonlit sky. "Lord, protect us all. Amen."

Brett ran around to the front of the building. He started pounding on the door and screaming at the top of his lungs.

"Vestuti, it's Brett Davies. Open up, I need to talk to you. Open

this door, Vestuti. You heard me. Where's Jenny? I know you're in there. Open this door."

A shadowy figure emerged from the darkness. It was Vestuti. The first part of the plan was in place. He came to the door as Brett continued to pound and yell. Glaring at Brett, he shouted back, "What are you doing here, punk? You and your players, and your stupid girlfriend, all trying to ruin me. Squealing to the paper and now the cops. Go away, leave me alone."

Brett didn't back down. "I'm not leaving," he yelled, confident that Chuck and Darnell could hear him, maybe Jenny, too. "Let me in. Where's Jenny? She was last seen outside the bank with you. Where is she?"

Vestuti flashed an evil smile at Brett. Opening the door, he glanced out into the parking lot and street, searching for approaching traffic. "Get in here, Davies. Maybe I'll tell you." Brett stepped inside. Arnie was nowhere in sight. "You don't need to worry about your little girlfriend. You just make sure no cops show up until we're gone. You do that and everything will be fine. You don't, and you'll be sorry for the rest of your life."

Brett nodded. "Where is Jenny? I want to see her." *Darnell and Chuck should be inside by now.*

"Grab him, Arnie." A strong hand yanked Brett's arm behind his back. Then he felt the gun in his rib cage.

"I got him, boss. He ain't going nowhere."

"Take him back to the office and tie him up. We gotta get out of here, pronto."

Arnie hustled Brett to the back of the building, pushing him through the double doors leading to the warehouse area. Brett stumbled through the entrance, searching for some sign of Chuck or Darnell. He was followed by Arnie, who continued to press the gun into Brett's side. Vestuti joined them. "You stay here and keep him covered. I'll go get some more rope."

Out of the corner of his eye, Brett saw Chuck peering over some storage boxes. He was less than ten feet from Arnie. The two friends made eye contact. Chuck pointed to the other side of the room.

Brett nodded, hoping Arnie hadn't noticed. Taking a deep breath, Brett turned away from Chuck and shouted.

"Chuck, grab him. He's got a gun."

Arnie turned for a split second, looking in the direction Brett was yelling. That was all the time the Braves' hitting star needed. Flying out from behind the boxes, Chuck slammed into Arnie. The two crashed to the floor in a tangle of arms and legs.

Brett later remembered feeling the bullet even before he heard the gun go off. The hot lead tore threw his shoulder. He ignored the pain. *I've got to get Jenny.*

He struggled to reach the office door when he saw Vestuti running toward him. But the drug dealer was intercepted by one large angry football coach, who snatched up the startled crook and put him in a massive bear hug. Darnell had arrived. Chuck was sitting on top of a defenseless Arnie, pushing his face into the concrete floor.

"Go get Jenny, Brett," the Braves star ordered. "We've got these two under control and the cops are on the way. Looks like I better call an ambulance, too."

"That's probably a good idea." Clutching his shoulder, Brett pushed open the office door to see the most beautiful vision in the world. *Jenny was safe.* She was also crying.

"Brett, I heard the shot. Are you all right?"

Brett struggled to untie the ropes with his good arm. "Oh, babe, we were all so worried about you. I'm sorry this happened. I didn't . . ."

"I'm fine, Brett. They grabbed me as I was getting into my car. They told me to be quiet and no one would get hurt. I couldn't. . . *My God, Brett. You're bleeding."*

Chuck yelled into the room. "Jenny, bring those ropes out here so we can tie these two yahoos up before the police get here."

Brett looked at his blood-soaked shirt and felt a strange warmness overcoming him. "The cops are coming, Chuck?" His words began to slur.

"Just called them a few minutes ago. I already told you that once, old man. The medics, too. You said you could get anywhere in

Rome in ten minutes, so they should be here about now."

Jenny gave the ropes to Chuck and Darnell as she glared at her two former captors. "I swear if anything happens to Brett, I'll make sure both of you are in prison till your teeth rot out. *You two are scum.*"

Chuck motioned to Jenny. "Well said, young lady. But what you need to do right now is help Brett lie down and keep him still. Get that towel over there and tie it around his shoulder. We've got to stop the bleeding."

Jenny helped Brett sit down and lean against some storage racks. He surveyed the scene in front of him as Jenny worked to tie the towel around his wounded shoulder. Chuck and Darnell had the two thugs lying on the floor and had roped their hands and feet back-to-back.

"You want me to duct tape their mouths shut?" Darnell asked with a sly smile.

"Nah, let 'em whine. I can't wait to hear what they say when the cops get here. Brett, how you doing? You hang in there. Help will be here any minute. I called your dad, too. They'll meet us at the hospital."

Brett tried to respond but could only whisper. "Why are we going to the hospital? I'll be OK."

"Yeah, you're fine. We'll just put a band aid on it."

Jenny finished tying the towel over the open wound. She bent down and kissed him on the forehead.

"Hey, Chuck."

"Yeah, old man?"

"At least it's not my pitching shoulder."

Everyone, except the two crooks, laughed as the tension of the wild evening started to wane. It had been a very long day.

Brett closed his eyes to rest. He could feel the warmth of Jenny's hand holding his. She kissed him gently again, this time on his cheek. The sounds of laughter were welcoming. He thought he heard sirens approaching as he slipped into a dreamy unconsciousness.

19

HOME GAME

The noise of the large Sunday night crowd drifted down the long hallway between the locker room and the Atlanta Braves dugout. Brett stood there alone waiting for Chuck to join him. Looking down the corridor, he could see the glimmer of light leading to the field. In a few minutes, he would be out on the pitcher's mound in front of thousands of Braves fans and ESPN's nationally televised Sunday night audience. Jenny would be in the stands. She would be sitting in the Braves' family section behind their dugout, and his mother would be with her. Sarah, Darnell, Celia, and all their kids would be there, too. Dr. Jake and his family, part of Brett's family now, would be sitting near them with as many Back Creek Church staff, parents, and youth as Brett could get tickets for.

Brett adjusted his sling and winced. He could still feel the pain of the bullet entering his arm. Morey and Schulz had visited Brett in the hospital. They assured him he would have a place in the Braves' organization next year. And before they left, Morey spoke to Brett's mom, who was staying in the room with her son.

"Ms. Davies, there is one last thing we'd like Brett to do for us this season."

She gave the GM a questioning look as Brett listened. "What would that be, Mr. Morey?"

"We'd like you and the rest of Brett's family to be our guests at the Sunday night game with the Phillies." Morey turned to Brett.

"And young man, we want to recognize the heroism you, Chuck, and your friend Darnell showed in catching those criminals and rescuing Jenny. Plus, we want you to throw out the first pitch of the game for us that night."

He had just found out about the special ceremonies for Sunday night when Dr. Jake visited him in the hospital. "I really want you to come to the game, Dad." It still felt strange saying "Dad." Brett hoped he would get used to it.

"Thanks, Brett." The minister looked away for a brief second and then turned back to his oldest son. "You know, I tried to see as many of your games as possible while you were growing up. But I missed too many of them. I'm so sorry. I'm not missing this one."

Brett smiled at the memory. He could feel his nervousness growing as the moment neared for him to go on the field. *Where was Chuck?* He grimaced as he adjusted the sling supporting his wounded left arm. The bullet had gone cleanly through, and the surgeon had assured him that his shoulder would heal. But it still hurt.

The locker room door opened, and Chuck joined his friend in the hallway.

"Ready to get going, old man? You're throwing out the first pitch of the game in ten minutes. Can't keep ESPN and all your fans waiting, can we?"

"I guess I'm ready, Chuck. Tell you the truth, I'm really nervous. You'd think I was pitching in the real game."

Chuck smiled and pointed to Brett's left arm. "Not till that hole in your wing heals up. You gonna be able to throw a pitch to Billy with your arm in that sling? I mean, I know you're right-handed and all that, but I don't want you falling off to one side or anything."

"Very funny, once again, Chuck. I suppose we and our national TV audience will all find out at the same time." Brett gave his friend a pat on the back with his good arm. "At least it wasn't my pitching arm. Come on, let's go meet our fans."

They walked down the long corridor in silence. The crowd noise grew as they approached the dugout, the sights and smells of a major league ballpark getting nearer. Most of the Braves players were on the field getting some last-minute running and throwing in. Chuck went off to join his teammates. Brett took a seat alone in the dugout. He closed his eyes and thought back on the crazy events of the past two weeks... his trip to Albemarle, the church meeting, rescuing Jenny, the hospital. So much had happened, yet now he felt calm and at peace.

Brett's thoughts were interrupted as the Braves players started returning to the dugout and greeting their friend, the "hero." An assistant with ESPN sat down next to Brett and explained what he would need to do.

"Follow me over here, Brett. Here's what's going to happen. The PA announcer will introduce you, Chuck, and Darnell. You'll all walk to home plate, where you'll be joined by the Braves' TV guy, Monty Wagner. He'll read a statement from the organization recognizing all that you three did. Which, I might add, is pretty amazing. Anyway, when he's done with that, you do your pitching thing and that's it. Any questions?"

"Well, yes. Where's Darnell? And who gives me the baseball to throw?"

"I'm right behind you, Brett. As always, of course."

Brett turned around to see Darnell with a big grin on his face. "Wouldn't miss this for the world. I get to go out on the field and stand at home plate *in the Atlanta Braves' stadium.*"

"Better yet, you get to stand there with Brett and me. Doesn't get any better than that, does it?" Chuck had joined them now.

"Chuck, is Jenny here yet? What about the others? Did they all get their tickets?"

"Step out here on the field and see for yourself, old man. They're all here."

Brett walked out of the dugout and turned to face the stands. There was a growing murmur from the crowd as the Braves fans got their initial glimpse of their new hero. Brett saw his mother and Jenny first, then Chuck's and Darnell's families. Dr. Jake, along with Nancy, Justin, and Lisa, were waving to him, as were lots of Back

Creek parents, coaches, and players from Brett's baseball teams. They were all there.

Jenny waved to him, smiling as always. "Say hello to Mr. Brett, kids. *He's our hero.*"

In unison, little voices screamed out, *"Hi, Mr. Brett! You're our hero."* The fans around the Brett Davies cheering section laughed and applauded. Brett smiled and used his good arm to tip his Braves cap to his fans. It was perfect.

The ESPN assistant approached. "OK, gentlemen, it's show time. Follow me."

The large Sunday night crowd was cheering as the PA announcer spoke. Brett felt like he was walking in a fog. Somehow, he reached home plate, where Morey and Wagner were waiting, along with Brett's favorite catcher. Billy tossed him a baseball.

"Throw me one more strike. OK, Brett?"

"I'll try," Brett whispered, "but I hope my legs stop shaking."

Monty Wagner began reading from a prepared script, recounting the events of last Friday night in Rome. The crowd roared their appreciation. Players from both teams applauded as Darnell, Chuck, and finally Brett were recognized, and each given a plaque by Morey. Wagner was concluding his remarks.

"And now, I want all our Braves fans here in the stadium, plus those watching at home on ESPN, to join me in inviting our Rome Braves player and coach, Brett Davies, to the mound one more time to throw out the first pitch of the ball game."

The crowd's cheering grew even louder. Brett looked at his friends. "Don't make me go out there alone, guys. Come on, let's do this as a team."

Brett handed his plaque to Darnell and took the baseball Billy had given him out of his pocket. The three friends walked out to the mound together. Chuck and Darnell took up positions on either side of Brett as he strode to the pitching rubber, turned around, and faced Billy. He gazed up into the stands one more time to see his family and friends gathered behind the first base dugout. They were on their feet, cheering and applauding...Jenny, his mom, Dr.

Jake, all of them. Brett still wasn't sure what the future held for him, but somehow that didn't matter now. Whatever lay ahead, he had someone to share it with. Everything would be all right. He was finally home.

Brett toed the rubber and looked in at Billy as the crowd's applause echoed in his ears. Taking a deep breath, he stepped toward home plate and fired a perfect strike to his catcher. *Man, I love it when I can do that!*

CPSIA information can be obtained
at www.ICGtesting.com
Printed in the USA
LVHW111504121022
730557LV00005B/95